MW01701225

Captive Dawn

Book Twenty-One in the Redemption Mountain Historical Western Romance Series

SHIRLEEN DAVIES

Books Series by Shirleen Davies

Historical Western Romances

Redemption Mountain
MacLarens of Fire Mountain Historical
MacLarens of Boundary Mountain

Contemporary Western Romance

Cowboys of Whistle Rock Ranch
MacLarens of Fire Mountain Contemporary
Macklins of Whiskey Bend

Romantic Suspense

Eternal Brethren Military Romantic Suspense
Peregrine Bay Romantic Suspense

The best way to stay in touch is to subscribe to my newsletter. Go to my Website **www.shirleendavies.com** and fill in your email and name in the Join My Newsletter boxes. That's it!

For permission requests, contact the publisher.

Avalanche Ranch Press, LLC
PO Box 12618
Prescott, AZ 86304

Book design and conversions by Joseph Murray at 3rdplanetpublishing.com

Cover design by Sweet 'n Spicy Designs

ISBN: 978-1-947680-79-1

I care about quality, so if you find something in error, please contact me via email at
shirleen@shirleendavies.com

Description

He stole her life, her freedom, and future. Disappearing is the only way to get them back.

Thane MacLaren is the consummate cowboy. His life on the ranch he and his older brother, Bram, are building means everything to him. Catching and taming wild horses, fulfilling Army contracts, and working with the best ranch hands in western Montana is the perfect life. He has no plans to change, until an unconscious, beautiful young woman ends up on their doorstep.

Sophrona Sadie Thompson is on the run. Tired of being controlled by a family who cares nothing for her wishes and a man who only wants to control her, she disappears into the night with few belongings and less money. Her immediate plans are simple. Get as far away from her horrid situation as possible before she's caught.

Waking up in a strange home with people she's never met, Sadie can think of nothing except continuing her search for freedom. Knowing her liberty is at risk, and not wanting to put the generous family in danger, she must make a difficult decision—help the struggling new mother with baby twins or disappear.

Believing Sadie is to become important in his life, Thane does everything possible in his quest to keep her close. But threats from men who want to deliver her back to San Francisco persist, posing danger to more than just Sadie.

Will Sadie allow her fear to destroy a future with the man she's come to love? Or will she fight for the freedom to choose the life of her dreams?

Captive Dawn, book twenty-one in the Redemption Mountain historical western romance series, is a full-length novel with a guaranteed HEA and no cliffhanger.

Captive Dawn

Chapter One

Splendor, Montana
Spring 1873

The persistent raps on the hotel room door started again, as did the low, cajoling voices of the two men who'd followed her from San Francisco. Sophrona Thompson's gaze swung between the door and window, her one remaining means of escape. She had a decision to make.

"Open the door and talk to us, Miss Thompson. Your fiancé is waiting for word." The deep voice identified him as Everett Wardell.

Handsome and charming, few would suspect he operated as her fiancé's henchman. Wardell handled problems for the Crockett family. Big and small, according to Ezra Crockett, her fiancé, and youngest son of one of the most influential families in San Francisco.

So, she'd been reduced to being a problem. It didn't surprise Sadie, nor did she care. Running had been a bold yet unwise decision. She should've known Ezra would have his human dogs watching her. No doubt they'd known the moment she left the house for the railroad station.

"Miss Thompson. Please. Open the door so we may make plans for your return to Ezra."

Time to act. Allow Wardell and his compadre to take control...or run.

Stuffing her few belongings into the small, burlap satchel she'd used when fleeing, she slipped on her coat, gloves, and hat. Raising the window, she stared at the ground below. Thank goodness she'd taken a room on the second floor rather than the third as the concierge suggested.

Mumbling a quick prayer, she tossed the satchel out the window. Before losing her nerve, she drew up her skirt, turned around, and slid her legs outside, allowing them to dangle. With a yelp, she released her grip on the windowsill and dropped.

Landing with a jarring thud, she slumped to the ground, blinking several times to clear the ringing in her head. Sadie reached out, yanking the satchel close in preparation for her escape. Standing, she squelched a scream as pain radiated from her left ankle.

Determined not to be caught, she gripped the satchel against her chest before taking a few tentative steps. With each one, the pain receded a little more.

By the time she reached the end of the row of buildings, the confidence in her decision had returned. She still felt the sting of pain, but knew the injury to her ankle wasn't cause to scrap her plan of escape.

Using the short footbridge to cross the stream, her steps became more hurried. She knew it wouldn't be long before they discovered she'd left and came after her. Wardell hated delivering bad news to Ezra. He was paid to succeed, not let a mere woman escape from under his nose.

Moving along the water's edge, Sadie could feel her ankle grow heavy with swelling. She might regret it later, but for now, she'd grit her teeth and continue on. To where, she had no idea.

Perhaps she was being naïve, but right now, any place was better than being sent back to Ezra. Her stomach twisted at the thought of her tall, remarkedly handsome fiancé.

If looks could judge the man inside, he would've been considered a saint. Many people thought just that. He and his family gave hundreds to organizations that helped the poor. Those who were jobless and homeless.

How wrong they'd be. Sadie doubted he'd ever crossed the threshold of the soup kitchen or orphanage. He'd never sully himself by being seen with a crowd of dirty, whining children hovering about him.

Selfish and controlling, Ezra expected people to jump at any request. He wrote checks, making excuses for never visiting the causes he supported. The same organizations which would be critical if he were to ever run for office.

Stepping through a thick pocket of berry bushes, Sadie shuddered at the idea of Ezra becoming mayor of San Francisco. Or worse, the governor. She knew he had both positions in his sights.

An ear-piercing screech had her dropping to the ground. Lifting her head above the tops of the bushes, she looked around. The screech came again, causing her to duck back down. Heart pounding, Sadie searched the area, seeing nothing to alarm her.

Raising her head a second time, her eyes grew wide as a large white object flew toward her. It made no sound, passing within a foot of her before rising to perch in a nearby tree.

"An owl." Her whisper floated in the quiet night before being displaced with another screech.

Clutching the satchel to her chest, Sadie debated what to do next. She couldn't stay here, allowing Wardell to catch her. Given only one sensible choice, she settled on the best path, and charged out of the meager shelter.

Another ear-shattering screech pierced the night. Checking over her shoulder, Sadie spotted the owl still perched in the tree. Wincing at the pain in her left ankle, she shifted direction, hoping to be out of the owl's sight.

Listening, her heart began a more persistent beat. The sound of horses, their hooves pounding the ground, brought a new terror. Wardell and his partner were nearby.

Running as fast as her injured ankle would permit, she didn't slow down at the flash of lightning, followed several seconds later by a crack of thunder. The sky opened, the ensuing storm soaked through her clothing over a scant distance of a hundred yards.

Unable to see more than a few feet ahead of her, Sadie stopped beside a large pine tree to swipe water from her face. The action did little good. The tree's branches offered little protection, her bonnet long ago lost during her escape.

Squinting, she did her best to see through the curtain of water. With no idea of her location or which direction she'd run, Sadie's confidence at a successful escape faded.

No longer hearing the horses, she became desperate to find a dry place to wait out the storm. Unable to see into the distance, she stayed rooted in place for several long moments. When the rain slowed, she squinted at what appeared to be lights. A house? Maybe.

Staying out in the open would result in her capture and return to Ezra. That would never happen. Sadie refused to return to a man who held so little respect for women. He knew where to hurt a woman so no one noticed, how to destroy her self-esteem, making her doubt all her decisions. Not even her family believed him to be a cruel and brutal man. How had Ezra been able to hide his violent actions from hundreds of people?

Forcing her thoughts to her present dilemma, she studied the sky above her. Waiting any longer would make the journey across the open area more treacherous. If she could see ahead of her, Wardell could see her.

When the clouds concealed the moon, she clutched the satchel to her chest, blew out a fractured breath, and rushed out of her hiding place. The minutes stopped didn't work in favor of her ankle. The pain had increased tenfold, slowing her progress.

Her left foot landed in a hole, causing her to sprawl forward, whimpering in pain. Tears burned the back of her eyes. Rolling over, she hunkered down, touching the swollen area. She couldn't tell if it was broken, but thought not.

Glancing over her shoulder, she expected to see two riders coming toward her. Wardell with the familiar smirk on his face, and his companion. Her shoulders relaxed at the emptiness behind her.

Turning back, Sadie spotted the light she'd seen earlier at the same time the storm resumed its pounding beat. Already soaked through, she tried to pick up her pace, only to fight the sticky mud.

The harder it rained, the more difficult her steps became. Slowing, she kept her focus on the light ahead. Determined to never go back to San Francisco, she concentrated on moving one foot at a time. She lost a shoe to the thick mud, but didn't stop to retrieve it. Her goal was the light. Nothing could distract her from the golden glow ahead.

Body tiring, breaths coming in gasps, she lowered her head against the relentless rain. Exhaustion caused her steps to slow, but Sadie refused to give up.

Shivering, fatigue threatened to end her journey. Then she was there, staring up at the back door of a house. Six steps separated her from the warmth of a home. Just six steps and she'd be free.

Chapter Two

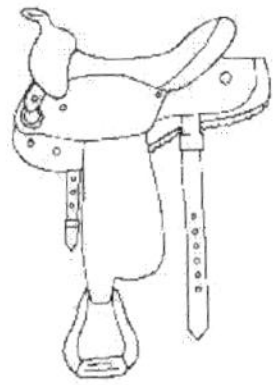

Thane MacLaren swallowed the last of his pancakes, tempted to ask his sister-in-law for a couple more. Selina wouldn't hesitate to cook up another dozen knowing the four men of the house would finish them off within a few minutes.

Selina's husband, and Thane's older brother, Bram, shoved his chair back. "Thanks, lass. Everything was wonderful." Lifting his plate, he set it in the sink before refilling his cup with coffee, his gaze landing on her extended belly. "How are you feeling?"

"Great. Good enough to go with you today."

"Not today, lass. We agreed you'd stay here until the baby comes. Shouldn't be long. A few weeks." Swallowing the last of his coffee, Bram wrapped his arms around his wife.

"If I'm going to stay here, I want to do something besides clean a house that's already clean." An accomplished horsewoman and rancher, she hated being relegated to inside work.

Up until a week earlier, Selina had accompanied Bram to Redemption's Edge, the ranch owned by Dax and Luke Pelletier. The partnership between the MacLarens and

Pelletiers to break and train horses for the Army continued to bring in substantial money.

"I'll keep you busy, Selina." Thane set his plate and cup next to Bram's in the sink. "Sun's coming up. I'd better get to the barn and see what needs our attention after last night's storm. I'll come back in to get you, Selina."

Their two ranch hands, Kevin and Vince Latham, had already ridden out to check on the herd of cattle. They were looking for a few more men to help with spring roundup. If they couldn't hire all they needed, Bram and Thane knew the Pelletiers would offer up a few of their men.

The MacLarens weren't used to competing against larger ranches, such as Redemption's Edge, for workers. After leaving their huge family ranch in California, the brothers had started over to build a presence in western Montana.

"I'll gather eggs and feed the chickens while waiting, Thane." She kissed Bram on the cheek before moving out of his arms. "I'll see you for supper."

"Aye, you will."

Thane slipped into a jacket as the sun's rays flashed across the eastern sky. The storm had passed, and he was anxious to see what, if any, damage it had caused.

Pressing his hat down, he grabbed well-used gloves before opening the back door. Thane stared down at the body sprawled up the steps.

"Bram!"

Kneeling down, he pushed damp hair from a face as white as the clouds overhead. Checking for a pulse, he let out a relieved breath.

"What is..." Bram's words died in his mouth at the sight. "Do you recognize her?"

"No." Pressing a hand to her forehead, Thane shot a look at his brother. "She's burning up. We need to get her inside." Positioning himself, he hefted Sadie into his arms while Bram held the door wide.

"Put the lass on the sofa. I'll get Selina."

"Have her bring blankets and dry clothes." Placing her on the sofa, Thane knelt down, once again touching a hand to her face. Sadie felt hotter than a moment earlier. This time, his gaze lingered on her pale face. He didn't doubt she'd be a beauty if she wasn't fighting for her life.

"Oh, my. Move aside, Thane. Bram, start a pot of tea while I get her out of these soaked clothes." Selina placed towels and clothes on the floor beside her as Bram dumped several blankets on a chair.

"I'll help him." Thane stood, taking one more glance at her before following his brother.

Selina's fingers moved deftly to remove the sodden clothes, dropping all but the undergarments on the floor. Using a towel, she ran it over Sadie's arms and legs before covering her with a thick, wool blanket.

Grabbing another towel, she wrapped it around long, flaxen curls, squeezing out the water. "You have gorgeous hair." Selina's movements stilled at Sadie's deep moan, her eyes fluttering open. Blinking, she tried to sit up, fighting Selina's attempts to push her back down.

Panic welled in Sadie's blue eyes. "He'll find me." Selina almost missed the rough croak.

"Who will find you?"

"I'm so cold..." Her body shivered, her voice slurring.

Grabbing another blanket, Selina placed it over Sadie's body. "What's your name?"

"Name?" Sadie's eyes closed without providing an answer.

"Here's the tea, lass." Bram set a cup on a nearby table.

Thane stood next to him, noting the color returning to her face. "How's she doing?"

"She woke for a minute before closing her eyes. She mentioned something about someone finding her."

"Did she say who would find her?" Bram asked.

"No. It could've been the fever talking. The tea should help." Placing a hand under Sadie's head, she began lifting before Thane took over.

"She would do better in a bed. I'll put her in my room for now." Checking to confirm the blanket was tucked around her, he lifted Sadie, taking the stairs slowly so as not to wake her.

Rushing past him, Selina straightened the disheveled covers. "I'm surprised she didn't wake up."

Placing her in the center of his bed, Thane touched her forehead. "She's still hot as a skillet."

"I'll prepare cool cloths. If the fever doesn't break, we may need to place her in the tub filled with tepid water or send for Doctor McCord." Selina rushed back downstairs, leaving the two men to watch over Sadie.

Bram crossed his arms, his gaze narrowing on their uninvited guest. "I wonder who the lass is."

"Maybe she came in on the afternoon stage. I can ride into town and ask around about her. Someone has to know something about her."

"If the fever doesn't break, you'll be bringing the doc back with you."

Giving a brisk nod, Thane didn't move when Selina returned with several cloths damp with cool water. "You boys need to leave us alone now. I'll let you know how she's doing."

It took a moment for the brothers to realize they were being kicked out of the room. Taking Thane's arm, Bram pulled him toward the stairs.

"We'll get the chores done. Selina should know by then if the fever's going to break. If not, you'll ride to town, and I'll head to the Pelletiers'. I'll work with the horses a while, then ride back."

Thane glanced around the living room, his mind moving in several directions. "I didn't see a buggy or horse outside."

"How else would she have gotten here?"

Brows bunching together, Thane's mouth twisted as he thought. "Walked from town?"

"In the rain?"

"She was soaked through. Her remaining shoe was caked with mud, as were all her clothes." Thane walked to the pile of garments Selina had removed from the woman. "I'll get these in the wash pan."

"Someone must be looking for her."

Thane stopped on his way to the kitchen and turned around. "Could she have run from a campsite?"

"Anything is possible." Bram's voice held more than a hint of confusion. "Why did the lass come here?"

"Might've seen the lanterns. I went back out after supper. Came inside about nine. Meaning she ended up on our steps between then and just before sunrise. That's a big span of time. It's a miracle she was still alive when I found her."

"Aye, lad." Bram raised his head at the sound of footfalls on the stairs. A tired Selina joined them.

"Her fever is down and she's asleep." She nodded at the bundle of clothes in Thane's hands. "Check for anything which could tell us who she is."

"I will." Thane walked through the kitchen to the mud room, where Selina did their laundry.

Dropping the pile into the sink, he picked up her dress first. Other than a coin purse, the pockets were empty. A quick search of the remaining clothes produced nothing.

"I'm riding to the Pelletier ranch, Thane. Are you ready to head for town?"

He held up the coin purse as he walked toward Bram. "This is all I found. I'll take it with me in case anyone in town recognizes it. Is Selina going to stay with her?"

"Aye. The woman hasn't opened her eyes again."

Thane shoved the leather wallet into a pocket. Walking into the living room, he glanced at the stairs as he grabbed his hat and jacket. Both he and Bram had a lot of work waiting for them. They didn't need a strange woman taking time away from what had to get done. When she was fit enough to travel, he'd use the buckboard to take her to town.

Bram had his horse saddled when Thane walked into the barn. "I'm going to ride with you to town. We can split up to ask about the woman."

"What about going to the Pelletier ranch?" Thane tacked up his horse, walking it outside.

"Dax and Luke will understand. I'll explain tomorrow."

Swinging into the saddle, Thane waited for Bram to join him. "I could use your help. Let's stop at the sheriff's office first. There isn't much Gabe Evans doesn't know about visitors to Splendor."

"Good idea. Gabe will most likely have some of his deputies help us out."

They fell silent for several minutes before Thane spoke. "What if no one knows her?"

Bram kept his gaze moving over the trail to town. He'd encountered a mountain lion, a bear, and a pair of outlaws determined to take his horse. Each time, he'd ridden away unscathed and wiser.

"Let's hope someone does."

"Agreed, but if no one does?" Thane shoved his hat down as a gust of wind crossed the trail.

"The lass will wake up and tell us who she is. By the look of her clothes, she's from an affluent family."

Thane shot a look at his brother and snorted. "Her clothes were ruined. How could you possibly figure they're high quality?"

Bram offered a knowing grin. "I spotted the label in her dress."

"You know women's clothes?"

"I recognized it from a dress shop Colin took Sarah to in San Francisco." Bram mentioned their oldest cousin and his wife. "When we'd have a good year, he'd order her a dress. This was after he took her there for several days to celebrate their anniversary."

"Do you think that's where she's from?"

"Could be. Or it could be someone bought the dress for her as a gift. We'll ask when the lass has had time to recover."

Thane's horse, Liberty, began to dance around. The gelding's ears were pinned back, warning Thane of danger. Bram's gelding, Bullet, reared back at the deep roar coming from their right.

Without a word, the men pulled their rifles from scabbards, aiming them at the source.

Chapter Three

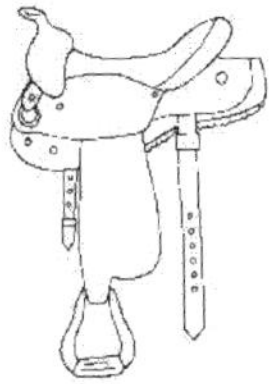

Splendor

"Where could it be?" Martha Van Plew placed fisted hands on her waist, her gaze narrowing as she scanned the one bedroom house. She'd moved from a two bedroom after her best friend, Angela, had married Shane Banderas the previous fall. "I know you're here somewhere."

Walking through her new home, she opened cupboards and drawers, knowing she'd never put away her parasol in one of those spaces. Plopping down on the sofa, she felt something stiff underneath her.

Shifting, Martha ran her hand between the back and seat of the sofa. Sure enough, the parasol had slid in the crack between the two.

Blowing out a breath in frustration, she slipped into a lightweight coat as a knock sounded on the front door. Without looking, she knew Cole Santori, a Splendor deputy, stood on her porch.

A sting of excitement landed in her stomach, then vanished. Their friendship had been unconventional from the start. They'd return to her house from what she considered a wonderful evening. He'd thank her, peck her cheek, then leave. Weeks might pass before she heard from him again.

Martha often wondered if he might be courting someone else, always shoving the thought away. In a small town such as Splendor, word of who was courting who would never be a secret.

After Angela and Shane married, Martha had traveled to San Francisco. The visit didn't last long. Being a single woman, with no contacts in the large city, quickly soured her excitement. The trip had lasted less than a month.

Upon her return, Cole had been quite attentive. They'd spent two to three evenings together for a month, then he'd backed away. Today's lunch would be the first time they'd been together for two weeks.

Picking up her reticule, she opened the door. "Hello, Cole." Stepping outside, she closed the door behind her.

"You look wonderful, Martha." To her ears, his compliment sounded obligatory as opposed to genuine praise.

"Thank you." She slipped her arm through his as they took the steps to the street. "It's so beautiful today."

He glanced around, as if noticing the clear sky and moderate temperature for the first time. "Yes, it is."

Cole guided them on a long walk around the streets until arriving at Suzanne's boardinghouse. "I hope the restaurant in here is all right." He sounded apologetic in a way she'd never heard from him.

A broad smile lit her face. "I love her food."

He didn't respond, though she noticed the relief in his features.

Suzanne joined them within seconds of them entering. "Martha and Cole. It's good to see the two of you."

They returned her greeting as she scanned the restaurant for a table. "We're unusually busy today."

"Because of the beautiful weather?"

"I believe that has a lot to do with it, Martha. Oh, look. A perfect table just opened up. Let me clear the dishes."

An awkward silence fell over them as Suzanne cleaned their table. Clearing her throat, Martha made an attempt to thaw the chill between them.

"Have you been quite busy, Cole?"

"No more than normal. Since Carrie and Griff married, the town has been quiet."

Yet she hadn't heard from him in two weeks. Perhaps it was time to continue as friends while entertaining the possibility of building a relationship with someone else. The idea didn't comfort her.

"All right." Suzanne motioned them to follow her. "Here you are. Coffee?"

"Yes, please." Martha and Cole answered in unison.

She handed them a piece of paper showing the options for lunch before leaving to fetch their coffees.

Scanning the menu, her gaze stopped on roasted goose with apple dressing. "Hmmm." She didn't know she'd hummed out loud until Cole lowered his menu to look at her.

"Find something you like?"

"I've never had goose."

"Then you should order it."

"I don't know. It's..." Her voice trailed off before she could mention it was the most expensive item on the menu.

Cole guessed what she had stopped herself from saying. "Order it, Martha. Who knows when you'll have another chance."

"What are you having?"

"The steak."

She knew the meat to be one of the least expensive choices. "That sounds good, too."

"Are you ready to order?"

Before Martha could respond, Cole ordered the goose for her and steak for him. "And save pie for both of us, Suzanne."

"Apple or lemon?"

He knew lemon to be one of Marth's favorites. "Two lemon please, Suzanne."

"I'll get these to you right away."

Martha watched Suzanne disappear into the kitchen before rounding on Cole. "You should've let me order for myself. I wanted the steak."

"No, you didn't. You wanted to try the goose. Now you can." He smiled, defrosting her icy comeback.

"Well, thank you, Cole."

"Tell me what you've been doing since we last saw each other."

She didn't remind him about the numerous times they'd seen each other since he'd last invited her to supper.

They'd nodded or waved, but neither had made the effort to push a conversation. Martha had decided if Cole enjoyed her company, he would've asked her out sooner.

"Let's see. I've become more active in the church ladies group. We're talking about opening a home for orphans. I'm quite involved in researching this idea."

"Does Splendor have many orphans?" He couldn't think of a single one.

"My understanding is we've been sending orphans to a home in Big Pine. Ruth Paige received a letter from the couple who manages the home. It's over capacity and can't accept any more. They want to send four orphans to Splendor, as they have no more beds."

"How big of a home does Ruth plan to build?"

"Oh, she's not planning to build anything. She wants to buy an existing house."

"Noah is the expert on what's available."

"Ruth has spoken to him. He was aware of one house south of town. It was built for three families, so there are eight bedrooms. According to Noah, the families abandoned it three years ago. The bank hasn't found a buyer."

"No surprise. There aren't many people who require eight bedrooms." He leaned back in his chair when Suzanne set down their plates.

"I'll get more coffee. Let me know if you want anything else before your pie."

"This looks wonderful, Suzanne." Martha's gaze moved over the sliced goose breast, her stomach rumbling its anticipation.

"Hope it tastes good. I've had many compliments today. There is one left from the man who brought them in."

"Does he live in Splendor, Suzanne?" Cole cut a piece of steak.

"No. He's a hunter. Travels all over, selling his game to whichever restaurants are nearby."

Cole swallowed the steak. "Which means he must hunt near large towns. I wonder why he'd come to Splendor."

"He knows your boss, Gabe Evans. Gabe provides a room at the St. James in exchange for being the first to look over what he has. The geese were brought down during the last few days during their migration north. He bought most of the birds for the St. James, but set aside a few for me. The Eagle's Nest restaurant sold all of theirs during last night's supper."

Martha had taken a few bites while Cole and Suzanne were talking. "This is wonderful."

"I'm glad you like it. Well, I'd better check the other tables."

"Interesting story about the hunter."

Cole nodded, taking another bite of his steak. "It is. Tell me more about your work on the home for orphans."

"I'm riding out with Ruth this afternoon to see the house. If it's suitable, we'll start fundraising efforts."

"What will you do if it isn't?"

Martha gave a slight shrug. "I don't know."

Neither spoke after Suzanne brought plates with large slices of lemon pie. Martha's thoughts were on her trip with Ruth, and how much good they could do if the house was appropriate. Taking the last bite, she set down her fork.

"Great as always." Cole slid his plate to the side. Reaching into a pocket, he removed several coins, placing them on the table. "Are you ready?"

"I am. Thank you, Cole."

Pulling out her chair, he again held out his arm. They took a different route back to her house, this time walking through Chinatown. Martha loved the various shops carrying goods not available in other Splendor stores.

"Do you shop in Chinatown often, Cole?"

"Not often at all. I buy vegetables from their grocery in the summer. The apothecary has an ointment which helps sore muscles. What about you?"

"The same as you. The owner of the apothecary speaks fairly good English. He's good at explaining the uses for his various items. There is a tea which helps me sleep. That is what generally brings me here."

Cole stopped in front of the apothecary. "Shall we take a look?"

"That would be wonderful. It will give me a chance to buy more of the tea."

The owner joined them within minutes, greeting them with a smile. "How I help you?"

"Do you recall the tea I like?"

"Yes, yes. I will get some." He wasn't gone long, returning with a small tin of tea leaves.

"Thank you, Mr. Chan. This is perfect."

"And you." He handed Cole a tin of ointment.

"Thank you." Cole was almost out of what he'd purchased a month ago.

Paying for their items, they continued out of Chinatown, turning left toward her house. Escorting her up the steps, he looked down, clearing his throat.

"I, um, don't know when I'll see you again, Martha. There's a trip I must make. It could take some time before my return."

She hadn't been prepared for this. "When will you leave?"

"Tomorrow."

"So soon?"

"I just learned about, well...I have to go right away."

"But you will return. Right?"

"I plan to."

"Where are you going?"

"New York, but I may have to stop in St. Louis. I'm being vague, and I am sorry for that." He reached out for her hand, squeezing lightly before letting go. "My time with you is the best part of being in Splendor. I'll miss you, Martha." Leaning forward, he brushed a kiss across her cheek. "I will do my best to return as soon as possible."

Turning, he took the few steps slowly, as if the burdened he carried weighed heavy on his shoulders. Martha felt his loss right away.

"Be safe, Cole. I'll look forward to your return."

Stopping, he took one more look at her before disappearing around a corner.

Chapter Four

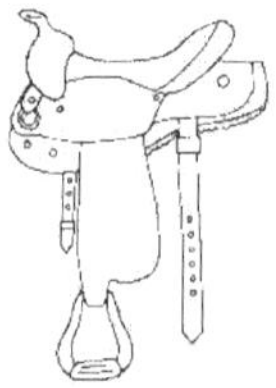

Selina pressed another cool cloth to Sadie's forehead and cheeks. Her temperature had decreased a little, though not enough. Leaving the cloth on her forehead, Selina picked up another one from the bucket, wringing it out before placing it at her nape.

Standing, Selina stretched her arms toward the ceiling. She felt every muscle after trudging up and down the stairs to change out the water and prepare more tea.

Placing both hands on her protruding stomach, the edges of Selina's mouth tipped upward. Her sister, Lydia, warned her the baby could come earlier than the estimated delivery date given to her by Doc McCord. She hoped her older sister was right.

"Where...am...I?" The rough words had Selina rushing back to the bed.

"Let me help you sit up."

Shoving away Selina's hands, Sadie pushed herself up to rest against the headboard. Swiping hair from her face, she looked around the room and scowled. Nothing looked familiar.

"Why am I here?"

Lowering herself to the bed, Selina adjusted her loose dress over her sprawling belly. “We found you outside the kitchen this morning. You were soaked through and unconscious.” Reaching out, Selina touched her fingers to Sadie’s forehead. “You aren’t as hot as when we found you. Do you remember anything?”

Blank eyes locked on Selina before images flashed through her mind. “Unconscious?”

“And ice cold. Do you remember anything?”

“I was running.”

“In the middle of the night?”

Pressing fingers to her temples, she closed her eyes. “Yes.”

Selina understood there could be numerous reasons a woman would take off in the middle of the night. Most involved some kind of threat, including fear for their lives.

“Was someone chasing you?”

Dropping her hands, Sadie stared at Selina without answering.

“What’s your name?”

“Sophrona, though I prefer Sadie.”

A smile crossed Selina’s face. “I’m Selina MacLaren. My husband, Bram, and brother-in-law, Thane, rode to town to get the doctor and ask around about you.”

Panic deepened the lines around Sadie’s eyes and mouth, her voice shrill. “No. They can’t say anything about me. He’ll find me.” Pushing off the covers, she stood, rocking as dizziness claimed her.

“Sit down, Sadie.” Selina’s voice was firm, yet gentle.

"I can't stay here. His men will find me and send me back."

"Where will you go? Do you plan to walk?"

Pressing a hand to her forehead, Sadie stood again. "I walked here, and I can walk out."

"What about clothes? Yours were ruined."

Sadie lowered her head to stare at the nightgown. "Is this yours?"

"Yes, but you're welcome to use it as long as necessary."

"If you'll loan me a skirt, blouse, and shoes, I'll get going. I'm putting you and your family in danger by being here."

"Why would there be danger?"

"The people after me will do anything to return me to my fiancé."

"Your fiancé?" Selina couldn't hide the surprise in her voice.

"My parents insisted I accept his marriage proposal. Nothing I said would change their minds. He's a horrible man. That's why I ran away. And that is why I must leave. Your family will be in danger as long as I'm here."

Crossing the room, Sadie opened the wardrobe and stepped back. "Oh. This isn't your room?"

"No. It's Thane's. He's my brother-in-law. I understand you'd rather leave, but you aren't going anywhere until Thane and my husband return. We'll talk over your situation and come to a decision."

Crossing her arms, Sadie glared at Selina. "The decision is mine, not yours."

"If I'm not mistaken, you have no clothes and no way to leave. Unless you're daft enough to walk out of here. Were you staying in town?"

Dropping her arms to her sides, Sadie's antagonism faded as she accepted her dilemma. "Yes. I came in on the stage from Salt Lake City. His men followed me from San Francisco. I thought I'd lost them, but I was wrong."

"They can't make you leave against your will."

Sadie blew out an unladylike snort. "They care nothing about what I want. Ezra pays them very well to do his bidding. I doubt he'll mind if I show up with a few scrapes and bruises."

Anger rippled through Selina at the image Sadie created of her fiancé. "Ezra won't care if they hurt you in the process of returning you to San Francisco?"

"Not as long as they don't mar my face or neck. Total control is all he cares about."

Selina wasn't sure what to say about the man Sadie described. She knew there were men out there who were cruel and brutal. Selina also knew there were many more who were kind and treated women with care. The men on the MacLaren and Pelletier ranches fit into the second group.

"Ezra's men also won't care who they hurt when fulfilling his orders. That's why I can't stay here."

"They have no idea what would await them if they come after you. Trust me. The men here aren't going to hand you over to the people you describe. You must be starving. I'll bring up some soup."

"If you let me wear some of your clothes, I'll go with you."

Selina studied her without moving toward her room to get clothes.

"I won't run."

A soft chuckle burst from Selina's lips. "That's good, because I'm in no condition to come after you." Walking to the bedroom she shared with Bram, she opened the wardrobe, selecting undergarments, a blouse, and skirt for Sadie. "These should fit you."

Taking the clothes from Selina's hand, she glanced at her extended belly. "How long before your baby is due?"

"According to my sister, it could be any time now. The doctor thinks I have a little longer. I'm hoping for sooner. I'll meet you downstairs in the kitchen."

Closing the door of her bedroom, Selina gripped the handrail as she made her way down, taking the stairs slowly. Sadie wouldn't be able to leave without her knowing.

Stoking the fire in the stove, she began warming a pot of chicken soup while thinking about what Sadie told her. Could the men after her pose a threat to her family? Were they searching for her now?

Stepping to the back door, she peered outside. She saw nothing other than Sadie's tracks. Did she leave other tracks the men could follow to the ranch?

Closing the door, her gaze landed on the scattergun a foot away. Beside it was the Sharps rifle Bram and Thane preferred. She knew Noah Brandt used a Sharps during the war. Those who'd seen him shoot were amazed at his deadly accuracy.

Selina still preferred the scattergun. Loaded with buckshot, she didn't have to worry much about hitting her target when they were less than twenty feet away. Hoping she didn't have to use them, Selina still checked both, confirming they were loaded and ready to fire.

"Have you used either of those?"

Turning, Selina nodded. "Both. I prefer the shotgun. Have you ever fired a gun?" Returning to the stove, she stirred the soup.

"Never. Perhaps it's time for me to learn."

"If what you say about the men coming after you is true, it would be a real good idea. It'd be best to have Thane or Bram teach you." Ladling soup into a bowl, she set it on the table. "Sit down and eat before it gets cold. I'll get you some bread."

"The soup should be plenty." Lowering herself into the wooden chair, she scraped the legs across the floor, wincing at the sound.

Slicing a thick portion of bread, Selina set it beside the soup before sitting down. Several minutes passed as Sadie ate, and Selina contemplated the young woman's predicament.

"Tell me more about the men who are after you."

"Not much to tell. Everett Wardell is Ezra's right hand man. He'll do whatever Ezra asks of him. He never questions the orders, and will do anything to look good in

Ezra's eyes." Setting down her spoon, she tore off a small piece of bread, taking a bite.

"I happened to enter Ezra's office one time when he and Everett were talking. Neither one noticed me standing by the door. They were talking about a man who'd died at Everett's hand. There was no emotion in either of their voices. Ezra said something about it being the cost of doing business in San Francisco. I'm certain he was talking about the dead man." Her stomach soured at the remembrance of what she'd seen. Pushing her plate away, Sadie tore off another small piece of bread, placing it in her mouth.

"He may have been speaking about someone else," Selina offered.

Sadie shook her head before swallowing the bread with a sip of tea. "Ezra isn't at all what he presents to the public. He's controlling and ruthless. And there's something else."

When she didn't continue, Selina placed a hand on Sadie's arm. "What is it?"

"I discovered he keeps a mistress."

Selina's mouth twisted in disgust. "Then you should call off the engagement."

"I've tried, but my parents insist I'm making an issue out of nothing."

"Nothing?" Selina's voice rose in indignation. "That's ridiculous."

"According to my parents and Ezra, it's quite common for a man of his social standing to keep a mistress. I don't care if he has another woman or not. All I want is for him to leave me alone."

"Why does he fight you on this?"

"Money."

"Money?" Although Selina thought she understood.

"My family is quite wealthy. Ezra and my father decided a marriage would benefit both families."

"Even if it made you miserable?"

"I doubt my desires ever entered Father's mind. Mother didn't even take my side." The misery on Sadie's face tugged at Selina's heart, making her angry at the parents who would put money before the happiness of their own daughter.

Placing clasped hands in her lap, Sadie stared down at them. "I know my parents love me."

Again, her heart squeezed. Selina couldn't miss the touch of doubt in her voice. "I'm sure they do."

At the sound of horses, Selina forced herself to stand, expecting to see Thane and Bram. Instead, there were two riders she didn't recognize.

"Quickly, Sadie." Selina motioned her to the window. "Do you know those men?"

Breath catching, Sadie began to shake. "Those are Ezra's men. I have to get out of here."

"You aren't going to run fast enough to get away. Follow me upstairs." Selina trudged to the stairs, inhaling deeply as she made the climb. "There's a perfect place for you to hide in one of the bedrooms."

She shoved open the door of the bedroom shared by their two ranch hands, Kevin and Vince. "This way. Help me move the wardrobe."

It took both of them to move the piece of furniture a little over a foot from the wall. Behind it was an unfinished opening.

"Get inside."

"You'll never be able to move the wardrobe back in place by yourself."

"I can do it. Now hurry. I need to get back downstairs." The words had barely left Selina's mouth when pounding sounded on one of the doors.

Straining to shove the wardrobe back against the wall, she stopped a moment to catch her breath. Returning downstairs, she stilled at the sound of the back door opening.

Chapter Five

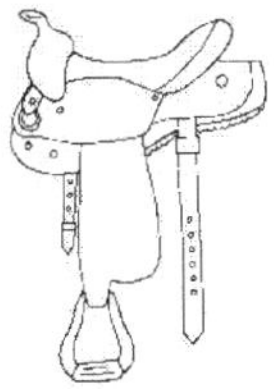

The men didn't announce themselves as heavy footsteps pounded on the wooden floor. Out of breath, and with her heart pounding, Selina moved around the staircase where they wouldn't see her.

"Maybe no one's here, Everett."

Selina recognized the name Sadie used for Ezra's hired hand. A man she wasn't in a hurry to meet.

"If Sophrona's here, she's hiding upstairs." The rough, gritty voice had to belong to Wardell.

Hearing his boot hit the bottom stair, Selina stepped from around the stairs, a .44 caliber six-shooter held with both hands.

"I'm going to ask one time for you to leave." The men whirled toward her, both going for the guns at their waist. "I wouldn't pull those if I were you."

The man with Wardell smirked. "You aren't thinking you can get both of us, are you?"

"I'm not *thinking* anything. I *know* you'll both be dead."

Wardell stepped in front of his partner. "We aren't here to hurt you."

"No? Then why did you come inside without an invitation?"

Taking a step toward Selina, he stopped when she trained the gun on his chest. Holding up both hands, he moved back.

"We're looking for someone."

"Who?"

"My sister. Her name's Sophrona. She took off yesterday and didn't come back. Have you seen her?"

"There's no Sophrona here. I'd recommend you two leave the same way you came in."

A slow grin appeared on Wardell's face. "If you don't mind, I'd rather look around. Just in case she snuck in when you weren't watching."

"I do mind. See, the thing is, my husband and brother-in-law are due back any time now. The MacLarens don't take kindly to men being where they aren't wanted."

Wardell's brow lifted. "MacLaren?"

"That's right."

"Any connection to the MacLarens east of San Francisco?"

"Why do you want to know?"

"Curious is all." Everett shot a look up the stairs. "My understanding is they have the largest ranch north of Los Angeles."

"I couldn't say, as I've never seen it. It's time you turn around and leave."

Wardell's eyes grew hard as they assessed her and the .44 caliber six-shooter in her hands. "You tell your husband

Everett Wardell came by. Let him know I work for Ezra Crockett. If he's part of the MacLarens in California, he'll recognize the name. You let him know we'll be back."

The glares both sent her didn't impress Selina. She'd faced outlaws and Crow raiding parties, could ride and shoot better than most men, and until now, wasn't afraid of men like Wardell. Being pregnant had changed her into a woman who'd do anything to protect her baby.

Following them to the back door, her gun never wavered. She stayed on the stoop as they mounted, spun their horses west, and rode off, all the while hoping Bram and Thane would return soon.

"Are they gone?"

Selina turned to find Sadie standing in the kitchen, body trembling enough to notice. Joining her inside, she set the gun on the counter, glancing outside one more time before closing the door.

"They're gone for now. I expect they'll be back."

Clasping her hands together, Sadie looked as if she could lose the small amount of soup she'd been able to get down. "Before your husband returns?"

"I don't know. Have you ever handled a gun?"

"Me?"

Selina cocked her head to one side without responding.

"No. I've never held a gun. Father said they were much too dangerous for women and most men."

"Out here, about everyone knows how to handle a rifle, shotgun, or six-shooter. Seems to me it's time you learned. I'll talk to Thane about teaching you."

"Why can't you do it?" Sadie looked away, embarrassed at her demanding tone. "I'm sorry, but couldn't you show me how to use a shotgun? If they return before your husband gets home, I'd be able to protect us."

Selina didn't have to ask to know Sadie had been shaken by the appearance of Wardell and his surly companion. Teaching her how to load and fire a scattergun might not be a bad idea.

"All right. There are boots over there that might fit you. You'll need socks, though." Selina rested both hands on her stomach while letting out a tired breath.

"I'll get them." Sadie moved toward the stairs.

"You can get a pair out of Thane's room."

The instant Sadie hurried up the stairs, Selina lowered herself into a chair, closing her eyes.

She felt more tired than normal. It was unusual for her to lay down during the day, but taking a nap sounded perfect right now. Between Sadie and the men searching for her, a few minutes of sleep wasn't smart.

Selina didn't know how much time had passed when someone shook her. Her eyes blinked several times as she raised her head from her folded arms resting on the table.

"I must've fallen asleep." On a sigh, she pushed up from the chair, surprised she'd nodded off. "Did you find the socks?"

Looking down at her feet, Sadie lifted her toes. "They're a little big."

Stifling a chuckle at the socks, which could've wrapped around Sadie's feet twice, Selina selected a pair of boots.

"These should be all right. I'll get ammunition while you put them on."

Placing a handful of shells in the pocket of her apron, Selina picked up the shotgun, and walked outside. Nervous about Wardell, she took a careful look around, knowing the men could be hiding in the bushes in the distance. Turning around, Selina grabbed the rifle. If Wardell showed again, both women would be armed.

"I'm ready."

"We'll practice at the other side of the barn." The location would allow Selina to keep watch on the direction the men had ridden off. The direction where Bram and Thane would be returning. She hoped they wouldn't run into Wardell on their way back.

"The description is similar to a woman who took a room here yesterday. She's on this floor." Thomas, the longtime concierge at the St. James hotel, motioned behind him. "I haven't seen her today, which isn't unusual. I've been working in the dining room, as well as here." He looked down at the counter. "Is there a problem?"

"We don't know," Thane answered. "This woman showed up at the ranch early this morning."

"Before sunrise," Bram added.

Thane nodded. "She was still unconscious when we left the ranch. We're just trying to find out if anyone is looking for her."

Thomas ran a finger down the list of customers, stopping partway down the page. "I could check her room, see if she's there?"

"We'd appreciate it, Thomas." Bram watched him disappear down a hallway behind them. Moments later, he reappeared, his features masked in confusion.

"There was no answer to my knock, so I checked inside. It didn't look as if she used the bed last night. The odd part is the bedroom window is open and the floor is dotted with puddles of water from last night's storm. I need to get someone to clean it up."

"Can you give us her name?" Thane asked.

Hesitating a moment, Thomas checked the name in the register. "Sophrona Thompson."

"Thanks, lad. Thane and I are going to check outside to see if there are tracks. Is the window still open?"

"Yes, it is. I'd appreciate it if you'd let me know what you find."

"We will, Thomas," Thane answered on his way outside with Bram in the lead.

Walking around the corner to the back of the hotel, their gazes searched the ground for any tracks. Both believed it would be a miracle if they found anything. The storm would've long ago washed away any tracks.

"There's the open window." Thane hurried toward it, checking the ground. About ready to give up, his gaze landed on a small print within a foot of the window. "Over here, Bram."

Crouching, the men studied the track. "It's about the size of the shoe she still wore," Bram said.

"There are more over here." Thane followed the prints. They were within inches of the back wall of the hotel. He came to a halt. "I can't find any beyond this point."

"I think we have what we came for, lad. I'm certain the woman is Sophrona Thompson. The tracks tell me she was running from someone. Let's tell Thomas and be on our way to the ranch. Perhaps the lass is awake and able to tell us more."

They stopped at the jail, letting Sheriff Gabe Evans know the woman's name before swinging by the clinic. The new doctor, Drake Ralston, finished with a family whose son had fallen from a tree, breaking an arm.

"Good morning, gentlemen. What can I do for you?"

Bram held out his hand. "Bram MacLaren. We met not long after you arrived in Splendor. This is my brother, Thane."

Accepting the outstretched hands, Drake grinned. "I remember. Your wife should be close to her time."

"Aye, she is, doctor. We have another problem. A woman showed up at our place before sunrise. Soaked clear through. She was unconscious when Thane and I left. Do you have time to ride out and check on her?"

"Doctor McCord is upstairs. Let me check with him." Rejoining them several minutes later, he held his black bag in one hand. "I'm ready."

Several miles passed before Drake spoke. "Tell me about the woman."

Bram glanced at Thane, nodding for him to answer. "We don't know much at all. I walked out not long before sunrise and she was sprawled out on the kitchen stoop."

"How old do you think she is?"

"Younger. Maybe eighteen. That's just a guess. She has fair skin, blue eyes, and blonde hair."

"Other than being out in the storm, did she appear to be healthy?"

"I suppose so." Thane scratched his jaw. "She wasn't too thin or heavy. Her clothes, though."

Drake lifted a brow. "What about them?"

"They looked expensive. She also took a room at the St. James, which costs more than the other places in town."

Giving a slight nod, Drake's gaze landed on the MacLaren house up ahead. "You think she comes from money?"

"Probably."

Brows drawing together, Thane thought of her clothes, the trimmed nails, the thick tresses. Yes, he was certain she came from money.

What puzzled him was the reason she jumped out of the hotel window and ran in the rain, collapsing at the base of the steps. Either someone was after her, or the woman truly was out of her mind.

Chapter Six

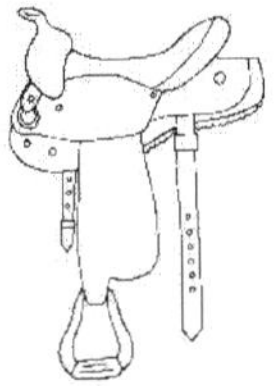

"Place the stock firmly against the soft skin of your shoulder. Aim and slap the trigger." Selina palmed a shotgun shell, handing it to Sadie. "You remember how to load this?"

"I think so." Her cheeks flamed when she fumbled with the shell, falling to the ground. Picking it up, she brushed off dirt and loaded the shotgun.

"Good. Now aim at the bush and fire."

Sadie did as Selina asked, tearing apart the leaves and thin branches of a bush. "I did it!" Her excitement had both of them grinning.

"Ugh." Selina doubled over at the pain in her stomach.

"Are you all right?" Sadie placed a hand on Selina's back. "Maybe you should sit down."

Straightening, she sucked in a slow breath, letting it out in an even whoosh. "I'm fine. You should do it again."

Sadie studied her, unsure about continuing. "Maybe we should wait a bit."

"Will you be able to shoot at a man?"

The question surprised Sadie. She hadn't thought about killing a person. "I don't know."

Selina gave an almost imperceptible nod. She understood Sadie's hesitancy. "If they return, the fact you have a shotgun may be enough."

Selina gripped her stomach, bending at the waist while groaning at the sharp pain. Reaching out, Selina gripped Sadie's outstretched hand, doing her best to straighten.

"Is it the baby?"

"I believe so. Though it's early." Her sister's warning that babies frequently come early flashed through Selina's mind.

With Sadie's help, she walked to the steps, grasping the handrail. Before she could move again, water dripped down her legs.

"What is that?" Sadie jumped away, her mouth gaping open.

"It's what happens not long before a baby is born. Help me up the stairs."

They made it as far as the kitchen table before Selina cried out, gritting her teeth as she reached out to grab the doorjamb.

"You aren't going to make it upstairs. Let's get you to the sofa." Sadie wrapped an arm around Selina's waist, steadying her as they walked. Helping her down, she assisted Selina in raising her legs onto the sofa. "What can I do?"

"I'm not sure. Some clean towels, blankets, hot wat...uuugh!"

She drew her legs up to ease the cramping in her stomach. When the contraction stopped, she opened her eyes to see Sadie watching her. "I'm all right. Please get what's needed."

"Yell if you need me."

"I will, Sadie. Thank you." Selina thought of the irony in their situation. She'd been tasked with watching over an unconscious Sadie. Now, it was Sadie taking care of her.

She didn't want to have the baby without Bram being present. He'd come from a large family, helping with more than one birth. Selina knew little about what to do during a human birth. Bram had tried to explain several times, but her pride had interrupted each time. After all, she'd been involved in birthing calves and foals. She now wished she'd paid more attention to what Bram had told her.

Selina tried to focus on something other than the pain. Would they have a boy or a girl? Bram said he didn't care. Neither did Selina.

They'd talked a few times about names. If they had a girl, he wanted to name her Audrey, after his mother. Selina thought it beautiful.

Agreeing on a boy's name was more difficult. Bram liked Gillis, after his father, who'd been murdered not long after the MacLaren family moved to California. The boy would be called Gil. Selina wasn't certain how she felt about it, though she'd offered no alternative.

"The water is heating." Sadie returned with the items Selina wanted, setting them on a table near the sofa. "Do you want a blanket over you?" She grabbed the larger one, holding it up.

"I'm warm enough for now." Selina's features twisted, her fingers curled into the apron as her knuckles turned white on another contraction. A loud, strained groan left her lips at the same time her eyes pinched closed.

Sadie watched, helpless to do anything. Hurrying into the kitchen, she grabbed a clean cloth, dipping it into the water on the stove. Wringing it out, she rushed back to the living room, taking a seat on the edge of the sofa. Using the cloth, she dabbed the wetness from Selina's face.

Folding the cloth, Sadie pressed it to her forehead. "I'm going to get you some water."

"No. I'm fine."

"I'm tired of hearing you say you're fine when it's obvious you're no such thing. I'll be right back."

Sadie grabbed a cup from the counter, filling it with well water from a pitcher. Returning, she almost dropped the cup on a heart-stopping cry.

Rushing to the sofa, she gripped one of Selina's hands, gritting her teeth at the strength of the woman's fingers. When the contraction stopped, Sadie picked up the cup, holding it to Selina's lips.

"Not too much." She moved the cup away after a few sips. "The contractions seem to be coming closer together."

"They are. It's normal. At least that's what my sister, Lydia, told me." Selina's features began to twist as another contraction gripped her. She held in a scream as long as she could before it escaped.

"Did you hear that?" Bram shot a worried look at Thane as the three men approached the house. He didn't wait for an answer before kicking his horse into a gallop.

Thane and Doc Ralston followed right behind him as another agonized scream reached them. Reining up at the back of the house, the three ran inside, the doctor carrying his medical bag.

Hearing boots slam against the floor, Sadie stood, whirling toward the kitchen. Her body tensed at the sight of three men she didn't recognize.

"Who are you?"

"I'm Bram. Selina's husband." Moving past Sadie, he knelt beside the sofa. "Selina?"

"Hmmm..."

"She's already exhausted, Bram. Let me check her." Drake set his bag on the table, bending to place a hand on her forehead. "Selina?"

Her eyes peeled open, then went wide as another contraction had her features contorting. Her gaze flicked from Drake to land on her husband.

"Bram!" The scream caught them all by surprise.

"We need to get her upstairs." Drake picked up towels, holding them under his arm while Bram lifted Selina and Thane carried the bowl of water.

Sliding her onto the bed, Bram stared down at the woman he loved above his own life. He hated seeing her in such pain. Eyes wide, her hand gripped the covers as another contraction sliced through her. The agony in her loud groan had Thane taking a step back to stand next to Sadie. She studied him a moment in silence.

"You must be the brother. The one who found me." Her accusatory tone didn't bother him.

"Thane MacLaren. And you are?"

She hesitated, watching the doctor remove supplies from his bag. "Sadie."

"Short for Sophrona?"

She jumped away as if bitten. "How'd you know?"

"Wasn't hard. We spoke to someone who works at the St. James hotel." Another head-splitting scream had him moving closer to the bedroom door.

"Bram, Thane. Please wait downstairs. This young woman can stay to help me." Drake dipped a cloth into the water, pressing it against Selina's flushed face.

As if seeing him for the first time, Selina's last scream twisted into a glare. "Who are you? Where's Doctor McCord?"

"I'm Doctor Ralston. We met briefly when you came to the clinic to see Clay."

Features going slack, Selina gave a jerky nod. She did recall a new doctor. "Does it always hurt like this?"

"I'm afraid it does for most women. You're doing real well, Selina."

She snorted, as if not sure she believed him. "How much longer?"

"Until the baby comes." Drake drew a chair next to the bed, giving her a knowing grin. "Babies come when they're ready. Did Clay tell you to expect twins?"

"He mentioned it was a possibility." Her gaze cut to Sadie, then the closed door. She wanted Bram with her.

"It's more than a possibility. Sadie, please take my place here. And be ready. It won't be long now."

Heart pounding, she offered a curt nod, taking the cloth from his hand. "What shall I do?"

"Selina is having twins." Drake went on to explain her duties. "It will move quickly. Can you do what I need?"

She wanted to scream 'no'. Instead, Sadie straightened, lifting her chin. "Yes."

"Excellent."

Bram paced the living room, stopping to look out a window before running both hands through his hair as another scream wafted from upstairs. It had been almost half an hour since he and Thane had left the bedroom at Drake's request.

"Don't do it, Bram." Thane leaned back in a chair, crossing one leg over the other at the ankles.

"What?"

"I can see you'd like to run back upstairs. The doc won't appreciate you interfering."

Jaw tightening, Bram resumed his pacing. His younger brother knew him too well.

"What do you think of her?"

Stopping, Bram stared at Thane. "Who?"

"Sadie."

Scrubbing a hand over his face, Bram stared as if Thane had lost his mind. “I’ve not had time to think about the lass.”

“I like her.”

“How would you know after less than an hour around her?”

Thane glanced up the stairs at another loud groan, ready to jump from the chair to restrain Bram. Relaxing when his brother continued pacing, he leaned forward, resting his hands on his knees.

“There’s something about her.”

He was stopped from saying more when the cry of a baby had both men rushing toward the stairs. Before they could start up, a second cry joined the first.

Bram shot a look at Thane, his brows drawn in confusion. “Did you hear, uh...”

Thane’s wide eyes stared upward. “Two babies?”

“Bram?” Drake stood at the upstairs railing, looking down at them. “Come meet your daughter. And your son.”

Chapter Seven

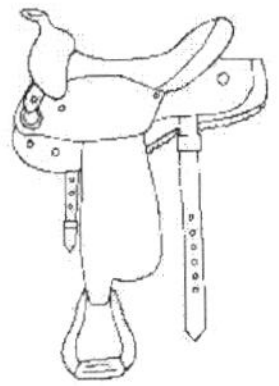

Martha Van Plew walked without thought along the main street of Splendor, her thoughts on Cole Santori and his quick exit from town. They'd been friends for a few months, so she didn't expect him to confide in her. Well, maybe she hoped he would have before leaving town.

She hadn't been able to make sense of what he'd told her. His explanation had been incomplete and disjointed. In truth, Martha had no idea if he'd return to Splendor. If he did, would he still be interested in a friendship?

Cringing on the last, she chastised herself. In the months he'd taken her for a walk and a meal, Cole had never mentioned courting her. Perhaps he never planned to.

Spotting Angela outside of McCall's, she held up her hand in greeting. It had been over a week since her friend had traveled to town with her husband, Shane Banderas.

They lived in a wonderful cabin outside of Splendor. Martha wasn't sure how her citified friend coped with being so far from town, yet Angela seemed to be thriving.

"How are you?" Smiling, Martha hugged her friend.

"Wonderful." Angela stepped back, studying the woman who'd traveled from Boston with her. "What's wrong? And don't say nothing because I won't believe you."

Tears burned at the back of her eyes. Looking away, she fought the urge to let them fall.

"What is it, Martha?"

"It's Cole."

"I thought as much. How long has it been this time?"

Angela had urged her to speak to him about their friendship and if he thought they had a future. She didn't like the way he went weeks without speaking to Martha, then showed up expecting her to ignore other plans to spend time with him.

"We had lunch a couple days ago. He left town yesterday."

"Did Gabe send him to Big Pine? I know he does that rather often."

"No. This has nothing to do with Gabe or Splendor…or me." The following chuckle held no humor. "He's gone. I've no idea when, or if, he'll return." Swiping away an errant tear, she tried to smile, failing miserably.

Slipping her arm through Martha's, Angela steered them toward the Eagle's Nest restaurant. "What you need is a strong cup of tea and one of May's scones."

Martha didn't argue, though she had no appetite. Seeing the distress on both the women's faces, Thomas selected a table in a quiet area of the restaurant.

"Your special tea and two of May's scones, Thomas."

"I'll get them right away, Mrs. Banderas."

They didn't talk until he returned with their orders. "Here you are. Please let me know if I can bring more of either."

"All right, Martha. Tell me everything."

Everett Wardell stood by himself at the Dixie's long bar, tossing back the second whiskey of the evening. It had been a frustrating search for an elusive woman who continued to confound the seasoned hunter. Easy to follow. Hard to catch.

His pride stung at the knowledge a young, naïve woman could lead him on a chase across several states, drawing him to a town in the Montana Territory. Lifting his empty glass, Everett ordered his third whiskey. An unusual act by a man who prided himself on relentless self-control.

Across the room sat his partner. The card game had been going on for at least two hours, and Hugo Pratt hadn't moved from his seat. On a good day, he'd walk away with four to five times the amount in his pockets. A bad day would still find him at least two hundred percent ahead. The man had a way with cards and knew when to walk away.

Which is what Everett wanted Hugo to do now. They'd planned to have supper at the Eagle's Nest, located in the St. James. His stomach had started growling thirty minutes earlier, signaling it was time for the elk steak, potatoes, and lemon pie he'd seen on the list for tonight.

He blamed his restlessness on the fact Ezra Crockett still hadn't replied to the telegram he'd sent several hours earlier. Everett informed him they'd found Sadie at a ranch not far west of Splendor. He knew how he'd handle the job. Grab the girl when she was unattended and deliver her back to San Francisco.

Everett expected Ezra might have another idea. His boss possessed an uncanny ability to come up with solutions which worked. No doubt this would be one of those times.

"I've been looking all over for you, Mr. Wardell."

Everett looked down at the wiry man from the telegraph office, who bounced on the balls of his boots. What was his name?

"Mr. Griggs?"

"Yep. That's me. This was marked urgent." Bernie handed over the telegram. "Knew you'd want to see it."

Handing Bernie a coin, Everett took the message. "Thank you, Mr. Griggs. May I offer you a drink?"

Still bouncing up and down, his gaze jerked around the saloon. "Nothing for me. I'd best get going. Lots to do before going home."

A rare grin momentarily brightened Everett's face before he opened the telegram. A frown appeared as his brows furrowed in confusion.

"What the..." he muttered to himself, rereading the long message to make sure he understood. "Pinkertons?"

Ezra wanted Everett and Hugo to keep watch on the ranch until a Pinkerton agent arrived. Frank Peacock would take Sadie into custody on the perceived crime of stealing money from Ezra. It was pure fantasy, a fabricated crime to quietly get her out of Splendor and back to San Francisco for a trial which would never take place. Everett had to smile at the simple beauty of the plan.

He glanced over at Hugo, who had his full attention focused on the game. Everett knew better. Hugo could play cards while knowing the exact location of everyone in the saloon, including what kind of weapon they carried. His partner would appreciate Ezra's plan.

Finishing his drink, Everett wandered over to the table. Hugo held a good hand. Once it played out, they'd walk the short distance to the Eagle's Nest, and over a superb meal, the two men would discuss plans to keep watch on Sophrona Thompson until Peacock arrived.

It would soon be over. They could put Splendor behind them while Sadie learned the consequences of betraying a man such as Ezra Crockett.

Thane leaned against the corral fence, taking a moment to watch Sadie empty a pan of cold water on the ground. He knew she'd been upstairs, helping Selina, while he and Bram had tended to chores around the ranch. They'd be riding out soon to help Kevin and Vince drive the herd to a location closer to the house.

Looking up, Sadie shoved hair from her face, clear blue eyes meeting his. She didn't look away as some women would.

Pushing away from the fence, he stalked toward her, slowing his pace to stop a few feet away. "How are you doing?"

"Me? Fine. It's Selina who's exhausted. She gets almost no sleep. Feeds one baby, then the other's hungry. She lays down for about two hours and it starts again."

"It's only been two nights." Thane winced at the comment.

"That's my point. Bram gets up, too, but she usually shoos him back to bed so he'll be rested for the morning. If she's exhausted now, how's she going to be in a week or month?"

"I'm sure I don't know. It's good you're here, Sadie."

"I can't stay."

Her statement hung between them for several moments before Thane broke the silence. "Have you ever seen a young colt?" He loved the way her eyes widened.

"Never."

"Come with me."

They walked next to each other toward the barn, neither mentioning her comment about not staying. Thane didn't know anything except what Sadie told them about the men who came to the house. He did understand the danger the men posed.

Thane admired her determination to escape her fiancé and the men sent to catch her. He wanted to know more about what happened in San Francisco to cause her to run.

"He should be in the pasture behind the barn with his mother. Right through those doors." He motioned her before him.

"Oh, my." Sadie moved to the fence, stepping onto the bottom rung to get a better look. "He's gorgeous."

"If all goes right, he'll be an important part of our horse breeding program."

"I thought you raised cattle."

"We do. We also breed horses."

"Have you been doing both long?"

Chuckling, Thane climbed onto the fence next to her. "My family has been doing this for generations."

Tearing her gaze away from the colt, she stepped to the ground. "Do you have relatives around here?"

"Not a one. We left Scotland when I was a young boy and ended up in California. My family has a large ranch there."

"Successful?"

"Yes." Thane stepped down beside her. "We came here to expand the horse breeding program."

"All the way from California?"

"It's not so far. You came from San Francisco, right?"

She glanced back at the colt as they entered the barn. "Yes." They continued in silence, emerging from the barn and walking toward the house. "I, um...ran away from my fiancé."

"I've heard that, Sadie. Why did you run?"

Wrapping both arms around her waist, she stopped at the bottom of the steps to the kitchen. "My fiancé isn't what he appears."

"Why not just end the engagement instead of leaving?"

"Ezra would never have allowed that."

"There you are, Sadie." Selina stood at the kitchen door looking haggard. "The twins are asleep. If you're going to be around, I'm going to lie down for a bit."

Bounding up the steps, she looked down at Thane. "Thank you for showing me the colt."

"Maybe next time we'll take a ride through part of the ranch."

The hint of a smile began to appear before her mouth stretched into a tight line. "I've never been on a horse."

His brows rose. Few people west of the Mississippi River had never been atop a horse. He settled his expression before Sadie noticed.

"You'll love it, Sadie." Selina stepped farther into the kitchen.

"I'll teach you how to ride and we'll take it slow." Thane wasn't sure why her acceptance of his invitation meant so much to him, other than the inexplicable need to spend more time with her.

She lowered her voice so Selina wouldn't hear. "You know I can't stay here much longer."

In his mind, Sadie wasn't going anywhere until those men no longer posed a threat. "So you said."

"I'm putting you and your family in danger, Thane. You should be glad I plan to leave."

"How do you plan to do that? Walk? You wouldn't make it far in any direction you'd choose."

Lifting her chin, she appeared to challenge him. "I'll figure out a way. I do have money. Although most of it is in the safe at the St. James. Perhaps we could ride into town so I may retrieve my belongings."

Resting a booted foot on the bottom step, he looked up at her. "Maybe. Once you are competent on a horse."

Crossing her arms, she rested a hip against the doorjamb. "How long will that take?"

"Well, now, that's a good question. We won't know until I see you ride."

The sound of approaching horses had Thane turning to see Kevin and Vince riding toward the house. Reining up, they dismounted, coming to a halt when they spotted a beautiful woman in the kitchen doorway.

Whipping off their hats, both nodded at her. "Ma'am."

"Sadie, these are our two ranch hands. Kevin and Vince Latham. Boys, this is Sadie Thompson. She'll be staying at the ranch for a while. Didn't think I'd see you both here today."

"Bram told us to come on in. He's not far behind. We drove the herd to the closest pasture." Vince looked at his brother, seeing him nod. "We'll ride back out in the morning. Unless you have a reason for us to go back after supper."

"Nope. I'd appreciate it if you'd feed the horses and check on the other animals."

Kevin settled his hat back on his head. "Yes, sir."

Before they grabbed the reins, a loud cry came from the window upstairs. A few seconds passed before a second cry joined the first.

"Bram told us Selina had twins." Kevin grinned at his brother. "A boy and a girl."

Thane glanced up the steps to find Sadie gone, guessing she was already upstairs with the twins. "The girl is Audrey. They haven't decided on the boy's name yet."

"Vincent is a great name." Vince laughed as he headed for the barn.

"Can't do better than Kevin." Grinning, he followed his brother, leaving Thane to head inside.

Standing in the center of the kitchen, Thane rested his hands on his hips. As exhausted as she was, Sadie had carved out time to make meals for the last couple days. He figured a night off from cooking would be welcome.

Heading outside, he grabbed what he needed from the root cellar. Onions, potatoes, carrots, cured bacon, and a small slab of salted beef. The burlap sack full, he walked up the steps, coming to a stop at the sound of loud voices.

"You should come with us now, Miss Sophrona. If you don't, the law will be out to arrest you for stealing jewelry from Ezra. He's a forgiving man, but you've pushed him too far this time."

Thane didn't wait for Sadie to respond. Dropping the sack, he drew his six-shooter as he exited the root cellar. To his relief, Kevin and Vince were walking up behind the two men on horseback. Thane leveled his gun at the one who'd been shouting.

"I don't know who you are, and don't really care. No one is leaving this ranch with you. I'd advise you to turn around and head back to wherever you came from."

"You a MacLaren?"

"I am."

"My name's Everett Wardell. This is Hugo Platt. We work for Ezra Crockett. You may have heard of him. His fiancée is in your house and he wants her back."

"I believe it's the lady's choice." Spotting Bram riding toward them, a rifle already in his hand, a slow grin curved the corners of Thane's mouth. "I'd suggest you forget your reason for coming and ride out. We don't want anyone to get hurt."

Wardell laughed, before glancing over his shoulder to see two men, their guns aimed at him and Hugo. Shifting in the saddle, he saw a fourth man about thirty yards away with his rifle leveled at him. No longer so confident, he faced Thane.

"You've won for now, MacLaren. Know that we'll be back, and the choice of handing her over will be taken from you."

Chapter Eight

"We need to learn more about her." The sun had set hours earlier. Selina and Sadie had put the twins down, then gone to bed. Bram sipped his coffee, keeping his voice low. "Wardell made it clear he's getting the law involved."

Thane stared into his cooling coffee on a slow nod. "We could send a telegram to Colin. He'll be able to learn more about Ezra Crockett. He might even know the man."

Colin MacLaren was the oldest of the cousins. Though two of the uncles were still alive, Colin managed both the cattle and horse breeding operations at the MacLaren ranch in California. He'd also been elected to serve on the town council with one of his uncles.

Bram's gaze moved to the stairs. "Can you go into town tomorrow and take care of it?"

"I can. Maybe I'll see Wardell and his buddy. I wouldn't mind learning more about them. They mentioned the law. The sheriff may know what they're talking about."

"Just be careful, Thane. Those men have no intention of leaving Splendor without Sadie."

"Don't worry. I'll be careful." Drinking the last of his coffee, he washed his cup. "I'm going to check the barn and corral before getting some sleep."

"I'll come with you."

"No need." Thane slipped into his jacket and gloves. "It won't take long. You should be upstairs with your wife and children."

"Aye, you're right."

Thane waited until Bram left the kitchen before heading to the door. Reaching out, his hand stopped within inches of the knob at Sadie's voice.

"I'm going with you tomorrow."

Turning to face her, his expression showed none of the irritation he felt. "Why?"

"Why do I want to go?"

"Yes. I won't be gone long, and Selina needs you here."

"I saw them, Thane. Wardell and Platt. I heard what they said." Clasping her hands in front of her, she stepped farther into the kitchen. "Being here is putting everyone in danger."

"So your real reason for riding to Splendor with me is to do what? Buy passage on the stagecoach and leave?"

Unable to meet his gaze, she stared at the floor. "I thought it a good idea."

Leaning a hip against the edge of the counter, he crossed his arms. "Where would you go?"

"South."

He couldn't contain a derisive snort. "South? Can you be more specific?"

Grabbing the back of a chair, the legs scraped against the wooden floor as she drew it toward her. Lowering herself, Sadie let out a distinctive sigh before looking at Thane.

"Maybe Denver?"

"All right. Once you reach Denver, where will you stay? Do you have money? You do understand Wardell will follow you. If Ezra is determined to get you back, you won't be able to get away from Wardell or Platt, Sadie. They'll chase you until there's nowhere else to go. Can't you see that?"

Resting her hands on the table, her attention moved to the faded paint on the walls, the gouges in the floor, and a crack in one window. All so different from her family home or Ezra's elegant mansion. Even with the flaws, there was more warmth in this house than any she'd known in San Francisco.

"What if something happened to the babies because of me? I'd never forgive myself." Leaning forward, the sincerity in her eyes pierced his chest. "It's better if I leave."

Studying her for a long moment, he dropped his arms, shifting toward the door. "I have to check the barn and our horses. Do you want to come with me?"

Surprise shown in her wide eyes before she shoved the chair back and stood. "Yes."

"It has turned chilly. You'll want to wear a jacket." Thane lifted one from a hook, handing it to her.

Without a word, she slipped it on before following him down the steps. Thane was right, the wind had picked up, whipping cold gusts at their faces. Other than the chill, the night was beautiful with a clear sky and few clouds.

Holding a lantern, he entered the barn, moving from one stall to the next. Double-checking the back doors, he gave a sharp nod when confirming they were secure. As he walked past Sadie, he felt her fingers dig into his arm.

"Please let me go with you in the morning, Thane. I can take the afternoon stage to Big Pine. Everyone will be safe with me gone."

Tugging his arm away, he continued to the storage room. "You're staying here with Selina."

"You can't force me to stay here. I'm not your prisoner."

"No, you aren't. You can leave any time."

"All right. May I borrow a wagon?"

"No."

Crossing her arms, she glared at him. "Why not?"

"We've none to spare."

"Then how am I going to leave?" She saw the hint of a smile curve his lips, causing her anger to rise as the meaning became clear. "You know I can't walk all the way to the next town. Selina told me it takes hours by horse."

"She's right. Longer by stagecoach. We should get back in the house. I'm more than ready to climb into bed." Motioning for her to proceed him up the steps, he froze for a split second as a bullet whizzed past his head to lodge next to the kitchen door.

Shoving a screaming Sadie down, he drew his six-shooter at the same time another bullet sliced the side of his head. Dizziness assailed him. He gripped the handrail.

"Stay down and get into the house, Sadie."

Turning to look at him, she shook her head. "You're bleeding. You need help."

"It's nothing. Go on." His head inclined toward the door. Touching the side of his head, his hand came away covered in blood. He worked to contain the waves of nausea and dizziness.

"All right, but you'd better be right behind me. That wound needs tending."

The kitchen door barely closed behind her before several more shots rang out, one breaking a window. A large chard fell toward him. If he hadn't looked up and rolled out of the way, the glass would've sliced down his torso.

Thane's breaths came in hard gasps. He needed to get into the house. Crawling up the steps, he froze at the sound of a repeating rifle coming from above him. A moment later, the blast of the scattergun confirmed Bram and Selina were providing him cover to get into the house. From the direction of the bunkhouse, two more blasts came in quick succession. Vince and Kevin had joined the fight.

"Come on, Thane." Sadie's voice and the slightly open kitchen door caused him to move.

Slipping on the slick steps, he found traction, hurling himself inside, taking Sadie down. Bram and Selina continued to fire their weapons.

"Get off me." Sadie pushed at his inert body, realizing he'd passed out. Shoving his shoulders, he groaned as blood trickled down his face and neck. Readying for a second attempt to roll from under him, she gasped as the weight was pulled from her. Bram stood above them, dropping on his knees to study Thane's injuries.

Sadie stood. "I'll get warm water and rags."

"We'll need a needle and thread, too."

Nodding, she dipped a towel into a pot of water on the stove, wringing it out before handing it to Bram. Rushing into the living room, she grabbed a needle and thread from Selina's sewing basket. Dropping to her knees next to Bram, she began to feel faint. Seeing the amount of blood, she thought they may have lost Thane.

"Is he..."

"He'll be fine. I'll take care of his wounds, Sadie. I'd appreciate it if you'd check on Selina and the twins upstairs."

Swallowing, she nodded before steadying herself against the doorjamb and heading upstairs. Selina held Audrey while stroking the hair of the baby's twin. Sadie swept up the whimpering boy into her arms, holding him against her chest until he calmed. Selina caught her gaze.

"Where's Bram?"

"He's tending to Thane. A bullet, well..." Sadie let out a shaky breath. "A bullet sliced across one side of his head. He has to sew it closed." She winced on the last, continuing to walk with the baby in her arms.

"Was it your friends?"

"They aren't friends of mine, Selina. I didn't see who was shooting, but don't know who else it would be. Unless you have enemies."

Selina shook her head. “None. Had to be Wardell and his partner. Your fiancé must want you back awfully bad.”

“It’s access to my family’s money he wants. I have to leave here. Surely you understand after this.” She walked toward the window.

“Stay back. They may still be out there.”

“It’s doubtful. I believe you, Bram, Vince, and Kev ran them off.” At least she hoped the shooters were gone.

With Thane down, Bram tending him, and Selina busy with the twins, now was the perfect time to grab a horse and ride off. Instead of acting on impulse, Sadie tossed aside the idea. Thane was right. She couldn’t leave Selina to deal with the twins alone.

But she has Bram. The thought didn’t change her mind. The ranch needed all four men to be a success. As frustrating as it was to admit, Selina needed her.

“You’d be no safer on your own. A young woman traveling alone would gather attention of the wrong type. If you stay, the men will protect you.”

“Do you think Thane and Bram’s relatives in California know Ezra?” Sadie tucked the baby boy closer to her.

“It’s possible. From what they say, their family is involved in community issues in their local area and San Francisco. Why?”

“No real reason.” Sadie’s tone said otherwise. Selina didn’t push.

“I’m so thankful you’re here. I could find a way to manage without you, but it would be much more difficult.”

Settling Audrey into her cradle, Selina stretched both arms toward the ceiling on a groan. "How is he doing?"

"He's ready for bed. You need to decide on a name for him."

"I know. Bram is firm on his selection."

"Which you don't like and he doesn't like yours."

"True. We'll decide soon."

Boots sounded on the upstairs hallway a moment before the bedroom door opened. Bram stood in the doorway, supporting Thane with an arm.

"I'm going to take him to see Doc in the morning. Kev and Vince will stay close."

"I don't need to see the doctor. It's a shallow wound, Bram."

"I'll send a telegram to Colin while we're there."

Thane shook his head in disgust, wincing at the flash of pain. "No need for both of us to go."

"Let's see how he feels in the morning, Bram." Selina sighed before it turned into a yawn.

"You should get to bed, lass."

She walked to him, pressing a hand against his chest. "Do you think the men are still out there?"

"Nay. Whoever shot at Thane is gone."

Sadie spoke up. "You know it had to be Wardell and his partner."

Bram nodded. "Aye. I'll talk to the sheriff about Wardell when I go to town tomorrow."

Worrying her bottom lip, Sadie considered her choices. There weren't many, and just one made sense.

Unfortunately, making sense put the MacLarens in danger due to her choices.

Chapter Nine

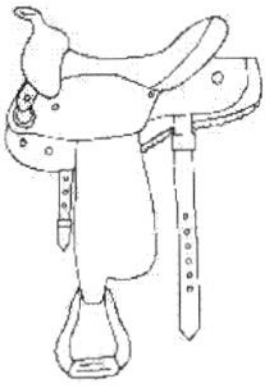

"That man," Angela hissed. "If he returns, I'm going to tell him exactly how I feel about the way he's treated you, Martha."

"Oh, no. You can't do that." Though she grinned as the words left her mouth.

"Of course I can. He's treated you poorly."

"I don't believe he sees it that way. I've decided he wants to be friends and nothing more. There isn't anything wrong with being friends."

"No, there isn't. Except I know you wanted more with him." Angela put a dab of butter on the next bite of scone. "These are the best scones. Better than those in Boston."

"That's because May is the world's best pastry chef. And she's right here in Splendor." Martha swallowed her last bite with tea, feeling so much better than when they'd entered the restaurant.

"What are you going to do, Martha?"

"I've decided to be open to other offers. The new doctor, Drake Ralston, is quite charming."

"And single," Angela said.

"Of course he's single. I wouldn't have mentioned him if he wasn't. Anyway, he would be a good choice. The new deputies are too young."

"They are entertaining."

Martha laughed. "Yes, they are. And handsome."

"Is being younger than you such a bad idea?"

Sipping her tea, Martha thought about it. "Maybe not. I don't know how old those boys are."

"Morgan Wheeler is twenty-six or twenty-seven. I know this because Shane said something about him being older than people thought. Jonas Taylor and Tucker Nolan are a little younger. So none of them are too young to consider."

Martha didn't answer right away. Cole being gone, maybe never returning, was becoming a reality.

"I'm not too interested in courting any man right now, Angie. I'd rather spend my time working with Ruth Paige on the home for orphans."

"You've always been wonderful with children. With the overflow in Big Pine, opening a house here is a perfect solution. Splendor is such a giving community. Why, it wouldn't surprise me if you raised the money for the home in one night."

"One night?"

"You told me the house you saw with Ruth would be perfect for the orphan home. The issue is paying for it and ongoing operations. You'll need to prepare a list of what's required to get through one year. Then we have a community supper and invite everyone. I will guarantee the evening will end with commitments for the first year."

"It will be a lot of work."

"But worth it, Martha. And it will keep you busy. Soon, you'll forget all about Cole Santori."

"It was stupid to go after Sophrona last night." Everett Wardell took another bite of his breakfast eggs. He'd been fuming since riding away from the MacLaren ranch. "We should've waited for the Pinkerton man to arrive."

Hugo Platt finished his slab of ham. Picking up his cooling cup of coffee, he leaned toward Everett.

"Capturing Sophrona before the agent gets here was a good idea."

Everett's brows drew together. "How do you figure? We left the ranch without her."

"The *idea* was a good one, Ev. How were we to know the MacLarens had ranch hands to help defend her? We should've reconnoitered before taking action."

Chagrined at the reminder he'd waved off Hugo's urging to take more time to examine the ranch and the number of people living there, Everett gave a slow nod. A colonel in the Union Army during the Civil War, Hugo had ample experience planning raids.

"It was supposed to be simple. Ride in at night and take Sophrona. But you're right. We should've planned better, waiting to grab her when she was alone, and the men were away from the ranch."

"I believe it would be best to wait for the Pinkerton agent." When Everett began to protest, Hugo held up his hand. "Ezra hired him for a reason. He never does anything without thinking it through."

"I don't like working with someone who's unknown to us." He caught the server's attention, ordering more coffee.

"He's already on his way. She's already proved to be more clever than I'd imagined. Finding a family to take her in was ingenious. The best way to get her home is arresting her. Ezra's set that in motion. I say we go with his plan. I'm anxious to finish this and get home."

Everett couldn't argue with the reasoning, though he hated to appear as if he'd failed.

"May I bring you anything more to eat?"

Hugh met the young woman's expectant gaze. "Nothing more for me, except a little more coffee."

She looked at Everett. "And for you, sir?"

"The same."

Before she could turn back toward the kitchen, an enormous blast rocked the windows and floors of the Eagle's Nest restaurant. Jumping up, both men drew their guns before rushing through the foyer to the front door.

Across the street, two men stood outside the bank, handkerchiefs covering their faces. Their hands held six-shooters.

"This isn't our problem, Hugo." Everett's warning was clear. His partner was a man of action, someone who stepped in at any sign of trouble.

Three more men, similar handkerchiefs tied over their faces, exited the bank. One held a bag of what appeared to be money. Before the robbers could mount their horses, shots rang out from all directions. Screams penetrated the thick air as one after another of the men crumbled to the ground.

Staying within the safety of the St. James entry, Everett and Hugo watched, wide-eyed at what took place outside in less than a minute. Several men holding rifles and six-shooters approached the inert bodies. At least three wore badges.

"I've never seen better shooting." Hugo couldn't pull his eyes away from the carnage. "If I didn't know Splendor was populated by ranchers, farmers, and shopkeepers, I'd believe they were professional shooters."

"We have a large number of former soldiers who know how to keep the town safe."

Hugo and Everett turned to see a somber Thomas, a longtime hotel employee, standing behind them.

"Sheriff Evans was a former Union officer. They train a few times a year." His expression changed. "May I get either of you anything else?"

"No, thank you, Thomas." Everett holstered his gun. "Please bill the meals to my room."

"Of course."

The sound of multiple horses drew their attention to the stagecoach entering the town. Pulling to a stop down the street, Everett started down the steps.

"Let's see if our Pinkerton agent is on the stage."

Standing aside as the travelers exited the stagecoach, their hopes were dashed when two women and an older man stepped to the ground. Hugo approached the driver before the man could enter the stage office.

"I'm looking for a man who was supposed to get off in Splendor. Agent Frank Peacock."

The driver's brows drew together, mouth twisting at the name. "Agent Peacock was gunned down in Big Pine. He left the stage to send a telegram and was confronted by two men. They shot him and rode away. Sheriff Parker Sterling organized a posse to go after them, but I don't know if they found the men. I had to leave to keep on schedule. Sorry to give you the news."

Hugo listened, his jaw going slack. "Thank you for letting me know."

"I'd suggest you send a telegram to Sheriff Sterling. He may have found the men who killed the agent."

Nodding, Hugo turned away. Everett would want to get a telegram off to Ezra right away.

"What'd the driver say?"

"Peacock was shot and killed in Big Pine."

Everett fell silent for a moment, working to control the frustration. "The driver is sure?"

“He is. Suggested we send a telegram to the sheriff in Big Pine to learn if the posse found the men who killed him.”

“A waste of time,” Everett spat out. “I need to let Ezra know. He isn’t going to be happy.”

Hugo shoved his hands into his pockets as they stepped inside the telegraph office. “Do you think he’ll call Pinkerton’s to send another agent?”

“Maybe.” Everett shook his head. “Probably.”

Several minutes later, having written and paid for the telegram, they left, wondering what they were going to do while waiting for Ezra’s response.

San Francisco

Ezra Crockett sliced a thick piece of steak, stuffing it into his mouth with none of the finesse most expected of the wealthy businessman. He’d been simmering since receiving the telegram from Everett an hour earlier.

Swallowing the oversized piece of meat with a little of his expensive wine, he reflected on the telegram he planned to send the Pinkerton Agency. An alternate idea had been building since receiving notice of the agent’s death.

Shoving his plate away, he sat back, sipping the wine while the idea grew. Pinkerton had accepted Ezra’s assertion Sophrona had stolen from him. Agent Peacock had been tasked to arrest and accompany her back to San Francisco.

"Why couldn't the sheriff of Splendor make the arrest and turn her over to Everett and Hugo?" His muttered question caught the attention of his server.

"Excuse me, sir. May I take your plate?"

"Yes, please."

"Dessert this evening?"

"Not tonight. I'll have more coffee. Put the meal on my account."

Walking to a nearby cart, he lifted a silver coffee carafe, filling Ezra's cup. "Anything else, sir?"

"Nothing else." Relaxing, he lit a cheroot, took a sip of coffee, and mentally composed a telegram to the sheriff of Splendor.

"Crockett, you and I have to talk."

Tensing at the familiar, gruff voice, Ezra didn't move. He said nothing as Malcom Sloan pulled out a chair, lowering his large bulk. Raising his hand, he signaled the server.

"Good evening, Mr. Sloan. May I get you anything?"

"Coffee and apple pie. Put them on Crockett's account."

The young man shot a nervous look at Ezra, receiving a slight nod. "Yes, sir."

Neither man spoke as a cup of coffee and slice of apple crumb pie were set before Malcom. Taking a bite, he hummed in approval. Picking up the cup, he drank over half the contents before pinning Ezra with an accusatory glare.

"There is ten thousand dollars missing from our account. Where is it?"

Stroking his short beard, Ezra shrugged. "We have expenses. I paid them."

Chewing another bite of pie, Malcom frowned. "I want to see the books. Both sets."

"There is just one set of books."

"Don't lie to me. You keep two."

"Well, Malcom, I'm aware of one," he lied. "It's on a shelf in my safe."

"What about the one you keep at your house?" Finishing his pie, he held up his empty cup toward the server. Once filled, he drank half of the best brew in San Francisco. "What did you do with the money, Ezra?"

"It takes money to run a lumberyard the size of ours. Payroll, inventory, the cost of delivering the wood."

Malcom's face reddened as his hands balled into fists. "I'm well aware of how to run a business." Shoving the chair back, he stood. "Let's go. I want to see the books."

"Now?"

"Yes, now." Malcom's voice rose, catching the attention of most in the restaurant.

"There's no reason to ruin an evening on accounting. This can wait until tomorrow morning."

"No, it can't." Reaching out, he was about to grab Ezra's collar when he tossed his napkin on the table and stood.

"Fine. But it's a waste of my time."

"It's not a waste of mine." Malcom ignored the stares of other diners as he walked to the exit. Tall, broad, and beefy, most looked away as he passed.

Behind him, Ezra stopped to greet people he knew, assuring them all was fine between him and his business partner. His heart pounded as they walked outside and crossed the street to the building he owned with Malcom.

They'd been partners in several ventures over the years. All profitable. The two still owned the largest lumberyard in the Bay Area, a real estate holding company, and construction firm. The last had built some of the most notable buildings downtown.

The arrangement had gone well until Ezra's spending couldn't keep up with his lavish tastes. He'd borrowed up to his limit, fired most of his personal staff, and begun appropriating money from their businesses in the hope Malcom would never find out. Ezra should've known his partner would discover the deception.

As they reached the building, Ezra stopped. "Let's go in through the back door. This lock has been causing me problems."

"Fine."

Reaching into a pocket to remove the key, Ezra touched a second item. His fingers curved around the handle of his .41 caliber Deringer. Sweat built across his brow as they approached the back of the building.

Turning the corner into an alley, he stopped at the bottom of the steps. No one except the two of them were visible.

“Why are you stopping? Let’s get this over with.”

Hearing the impatience in Malcom’s voice, and before he could stop himself, Ezra whirled around. Placing the Deringer against his partner’s heart, he pulled the trigger.

Chapter Ten

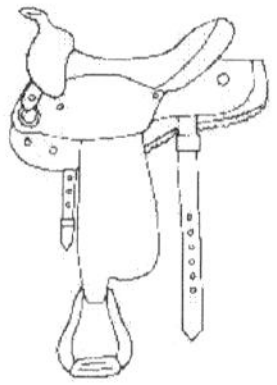

"Has to be wolves." Kevin walked around the carcass of a steer with the MacLaren brand. Several yards away lay another dead animal belonging to Bram and Thane. He pointed to a cluster of wolf tracks around what remained of the steers.

Vince tightened his grip on his rifle, surveying the area around them. "Not enough left to bury them, Kev."

Nodding in agreement, the older brother swung back into his saddle. "Let's check out the area. There have to be more tracks. We need to find the pack and drive them off."

Harder than it sounded, Vince thought as he reined his horse around to follow Kevin. They'd tried to run off a pack of six the previous spring without success. The fact this could be the same group of wolves crossed his mind. Perhaps they'd have better luck this time.

They crossed MacLaren land for two hours before stopping. The only tracks they'd identified belonged to elk and deer. There'd been a few piles of weeks old bear scat, but nothing to indicate a pack of wolves had passed in this direction.

The sun had begun its descent over the western mountains as the cold northern wind lashed his face.

Tugging the coat's collar tighter, he leaned toward his brother.

"We'd best head back, Kev."

"A few more minutes." Kicking his horse, he headed off toward a stand of trees to their right.

"Where are you going?" Vince's shout didn't make it more than a dozen yards.

The wind had increased, blowing gusts strong enough to dislodge a less competent rider from his horse. The gelding danced one way, then the other, before rearing back on its hind legs.

"Whoa, boy. It's all right." Vince continued the soothing words in a soft voice his gelding recognized. The horse continued to dance in fright before calming.

A crack of thunder turned his attention north. Dark gray clouds moved rapidly toward them. Vince searched the direction where Kevin had ridden, a thread of worry slicing through him when he didn't spot his brother.

Moving toward where he'd last seen Kevin, Vince shoved his hat down as a cold gust of wind whipped around him.

"Kev!" His shout disappeared as another burst of wind swept past him. "Kev!"

Hoping his brother had found shelter within a copse of thick brush among tall pines, he kept moving. Vince told himself he couldn't have gone far. It had been less than five minutes. Hadn't it?

Without warning, the wind stilled for several seconds before the sky opened. Rain pummeled him, soaking his pants while threatening to do the same for his coat. Picking up speed, he reined the gelding into the shelter of large pines.

"Kev!" He continued to shout several times without receiving a response.

Chest squeezing with worry, Vince directed the horse deeper into the woods. He stopped under the protection of a dense canopy of heavy pine branches. Removing his hat, he slapped it against a thigh before positioning it back on his head.

Thunder rocked the sky a few seconds before a flash of lightning shone through the trees. Shifting in the saddle, he studied the forest behind him. Vince couldn't recall ever being here. Considering the years he and Kevin had ridden for the MacLarens, it surprised him they hadn't noticed the large wooded area.

His body stiffened at an ear-piercing cry. If he didn't know better, Vince would believe a human baby was trapped in the forest. Instead, he drew his rifle from the scabbard. Somewhere close by, a mountain lion was hidden within the forest.

The cry came again, intensifying his concern. Had his brother been jumped by the predatory cat?

Positioning the butt of his rifle against his shoulder, his gaze swept the area around him. He hoped to see something, anything, that would point him toward his brother. Disappointment washed over him. There was no sign of Kevin or his horse.

Lowering the rifle, Vince scanned the ground around him before moving outward several feet. He continued expanding his circle, studying the soft dirt, knowing there'd be tracks if Kevin rode this way. Once again, acute disappointment gripped him. So did intense fear.

"Bram. Get over here."

Thane's shout had Bram running toward where his brother stood. Before reaching him, Thane took off at a run toward a rider hunched over the neck of his horse.

Even in the darkening sky, Bram recognized him. His gaze searched the area behind Vince for Kevin. Rushing to join them, Bram held out his arms when Vince slid from the saddle.

The ranch hand's clothes were soaked. "Where's Kev?" Thane took the reins of Vince's horse, leading the way to the barn.

"I don't know." The misery in his voice struck both MacLarens in the gut. "We were separated right before the storm came through. When it let up for a few minutes, he'd disappeared." Vince stopped, turning to face the open pastures beside the barn. "I spent hours looking for him before another storm opened up."

Thane placed Vince's horse in an open stall. Grabbing rags, he began wiping down the wet animal. "It was smart to come back here. We'll mount another search early tomorrow morning, right, Bram?"

"At dawn."

"I'll ask Sadie to put food together for us," Thane said.

Vince turned back toward them "We should take dry clothes and blankets. Kev will be cold and hungry when we find him."

Bram shot a look at Thane, who answered with an almost imperceptible nod. They believed the odds of finding Kevin alive were slim. Bad weather, lack of food and protection, wild animals, and unfriendly Indians raised the odds. It didn't mean they wouldn't do all they could to locate their friend. And nothing they'd do or say would burden Vince with their doubt. Bram let out a slow breath before facing him.

"You're right. Grab what you think he'll need, Vince. We leave at first light." Bram headed to the house, Thane not far behind him. They spoke for a few minutes in the kitchen before Vince entered the house, taking the stairs to his bedroom. All knew sleep would be elusive.

Splendor

"Take a look at what's coming into town, Suzanne."

The newest hire at the boardinghouse restaurant stared out the window as a procession of five wagons entered the town. Placing both hands on her hips, a wry smile formed.

"I've never seen a wagon train of all darkies."

Suzanne inched toward the window. "Frances, why don't you check on the pies. I'll bet those people are hungry."

"Sure. I'll take a look."

Watching as the tall, red-haired woman ambled to the kitchen, Suzanne found herself wondering if Splendor was the wagon train's destination or if they were passing through.

She'd always seen the growing frontier town as being at the end of the road. There were a few small settlements west of Splendor, but no real towns until arriving in Salt Lake City. Why her husband chose this place was never clear.

She considered leaving when he and their daughter died during a blizzard. By then, Splendor had become her home, a place holding memories of the two people she had loved more than anything.

"Pies look done to me. Want me to put them on the cooling rack?"

"That would be nice, Frances. And give the stew a good stirring, too." Removing her coat from its hook, she slipped into it before dawning a wool hat and stepping outside. Crossing the rutted and muddy street, she approached the driver of the lead wagon.

"Hello, sir. If you're hungry, I'm offering a solid meal and free pie at the boardinghouse. It's across the street, and there's plenty of room for all of you."

Tall, with curly hair graying at the ends, his piercing dark brown eyes locked on her. He seemed to be measuring her, as if wondering if he could believe her words.

"That's nice of you, ma'am. I'll pass the word around."

"You won't regret it, Mr...."

"Freeman."

"Nice meeting you. I'm Suzanne Barnett. I own the boardinghouse and restaurant."

A nod was his only reply before a young boy plowed into his legs and held tight. "Papa?"

"What is it, Frederick?"

Two wide, brown eyes looked up at him. "Mama says she wants you at the wagon."

"Tell her I'll be there soon."

Frederick stared up at Suzanne for several seconds before rushing off toward their wagon.

"I won't keep you, Mr. Freeman. Hope to see you and your family at lunch." Heading back the way she came, Suzanne could feel his eyes boring into her. Well, she'd made the offer. Now all she could do was wait.

Before she'd reached the kitchen, the front door opened as the Freeman family entered. Six people, two adults and four children, stood in a circle.

"Hello, Mr. Freeman. May I show you to a table?"

"Are you sure we can eat in here?" He placed an arm around his wife's shoulders, drawing her close.

"Quite sure. As I said, this is my place, and I'm glad to have you." Suzanne was making her decision known to both the people in the wagon train and the residents of Splendor. "How about a window table?"

"If you don't mind, near the back would be best."

Ushering them to another table, she indicated a round table with six chairs. "How's this?"

"It'll be fine. Thank you, ma'am." He and his wife hurried to get everyone settled.

"How about coffee for the adults and hot chocolate for the children, Mr. Freeman?"

"We'd appreciate it, ma'am."

Deep laughter came from the front of the restaurant. Heads turned to see two tall men, one wearing black pants, jacket, and vest over a white shirt. He wore a patch over his left eye. The other man was just as tall. He wore tan pants, blue chambray shirt, and brown cowboy hat. On his chest was pinned a badge. Suzanne hurried toward her husband and the sheriff.

"Hello, Nick." She turned her cheek toward him to receive a kiss. "You're a little earlier than usual."

"I know, sweetheart. But I recalled you saying the menu included venison stew, and I didn't want to miss it. Gabe thought the same."

"Other than a family from the wagon train, you two are the first locals to come in. And it's good you did. The venison stew is some of the best I've ever made." She smiled at their chuckles. "Take whatever table suits you while I get coffee."

Removing their hats, Nick and Gabe nodded in greeting to the family across the room before selecting a table near the window. "I heard Bram and Thane came to town," Nick said.

"A woman collapsed on their doorstep. They were trying to identify her. They got what was needed from Thomas."

Nick's brow raised. "At the St. James?"

"That's where she's staying. Two other men have been asking about her, also. They haven't been as open about their search as Bram and Thane. I've got a telegram off to the sheriff in San Francisco to find out if he knows them."

Suzanne delivered coffee and hot chocolate to the Freeman family before carrying the tray to Nick's table. "Here you are." She set coffee in front of them.

The slamming of the front door drew their attention to a short, wiry man with dark-rimmed glasses. Bernie Griggs, the manager of the Western Union office, rushed toward Gabe. Bouncing on the balls of his feet, he handed the sheriff a telegram.

"This just came for you Gabe. Thought you'd want to see it right away." Bernie waved him off when he reached into a pocket for a coin. "Not needed. I have to get back to the office."

Opening the telegram, Gabe's eyes widened at the contents. When finished, he handed it to Nick.

"Well, now. It seems those men from San Francisco have a colorful past," Nick said. "Says here to be wary of Everett Wardell and Hugo Platt. Seems you shouldn't trust them, Gabe." Folding the telegram, he handed it back.

Taking the paper, he tucked it into a pocket. “And I thought this might end up being a quiet spring.”

Chapter Eleven

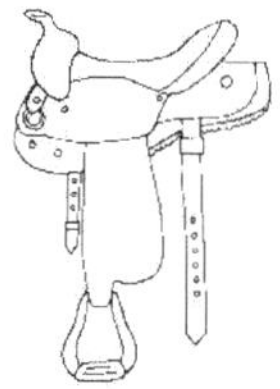

The trio moved through the dense scrub and pine, calling Kevin's name every few feet while searching for tracks. They'd left the ranch before sunrise, Vince carrying saddlebags loaded with food and extra clothes for his brother.

He'd seen the looks on the MacLaren brothers' faces. Bram and Thane didn't believe they'd find Kevin alive. Vince refused to accept their thinking. His brother was a resilient and clever man. If anyone could live through the previous night, staying warm and fighting off predators, it was Kevin.

Five hours later, having covered miles of MacLaren land, plus terrain outside their boundaries, Vince was losing faith. They'd brought provisions to stay overnight, but he knew Bram remained concerned about Selina and the twins, Audrey and Connor.

The two had agreed on the boy's name the previous night, minutes before Selina drifted into a deep sleep. Lying beside her, Bram brought the babies to her for feeding twice, rocking them to sleep before placing them in their cradles.

Dismounting for lunch, they pulled food from saddlebags after stretching their legs. "I'm not sure where to go next." Bram tore off a piece of jerky, looking at Vince. "What are you thinking, lad?"

"West, I think. Or maybe south. Heck, I don't know either." Vince bit off half a boiled egg, swallowing it down with water from his canteen. "I expected to find some sign of him by now."

Thane chewed a cold Johnny cake. "We'll find caves to the south. A good place to hide."

"How far are you thinking, lad?"

"A few miles, Bram. We can't do it today and still make it back home before dark."

Rubbing his face, Bram looked toward the ranch, now miles away.

"Vince and I can go south to check the caves. You could ride back to be with Selina and the twins."

"Nae, Thane. I'm going with you. Sadie is with Selina. I'll ride back tomorrow afternoon, even if we haven't found Kev. I don't want those men returning while we're gone."

Vince shifted to face him. "Maybe you should ride back now, Bram. If we don't find a trace of Kev by tomorrow at noon, Thane and I will head back." He tried, and failed, to hide the misery in his voice.

Unlike Thane and Bram, who had a massive family in California, Vince and Kevin had no family beyond themselves.

"I'll stay with you a bit longer. If you two are ready, let's go."

Everett Wardell read the most recent telegram from Ezra Crockett, his brows bunching together. Wadding up the missive into a tight ball, he tossed it between two buildings as he hurried along the boardwalk. Shoving open the doors to the Dixie saloon, he joined Hugo at a table.

"I ordered you a whiskey. What did the telegram say?"

"Ezra's sending another Pinkerton agent. He says we should expect him soon." Picking up the glass, he drank the contents in one swallow. "A waste of time. We should already be back in San Francisco."

Hugo picked up his glass, studying the amber liquid before setting it back down. "What we should do is leave this up to the Pinkerton agent and get back home. Ezra must have other business we can handle for him."

"I sent a message to Ezra asking him the same."

Hugo leaned forward. "And?"

"He hasn't responded." Everett signaled to the barmaid for two more whiskeys. "That girl has caused a lot of trouble. Ezra should let her go and find another woman."

"I agree, but that isn't going to happen. Ezra doesn't care about her. He's after her family's money." Hugo finished his whiskey in one swallow.

"There are other eligible and wealthy young women in San Francisco. He could even bring one out from the east."

"You know how Ezra is when he gets something in his head. Just accept it, Ev. It'll be a lot easier for us. It's not so bad. We're staying at a hotel with better food than what we get at some of San Francisco's finest. The Palace has decent entertainment, and we're a few hours' ride from Big Pine. Thomas told me there are two more places like the Palace and several more saloons there. I say we relax until the Pinkerton agent gets here and let Ezra pay for everything."

"You may be right." Waving one of the barmaids over, Everett ordered two more whiskeys. "No sense fighting what won't change." Yet he couldn't find it within himself to settle for sitting around and waiting.

"Let's join the table over there and use Ezra's money to play cards."

Rising, Everett picked up his glass. "That's the best idea you've had in days, Hugo."

Deputy Cole Santori stared out the window of the Wild Rose saloon, rolling the glass of whiskey between his fingers. The letter which had changed his plans, his entire life, was secure in the pocket of his shirt.

It had arrived a few days before Christmas. He hadn't seen the person who sent the letter for years, believed their days of being cordial were over. Perhaps because he wanted them to be.

He'd grown up the youngest of eight children in a wealthy Italian family. By the age of twelve, Cole craved a different life, something without the rules and restrictions imposed by a domineering father and uninvolved mother.

As a child, he'd snuck out of their New York City mansion as often as he could. He'd taken up with a group of boys from the *other side*, as his father called them. Children who knew how to have fun by running around the docks, stealing the occasional apple, and peeking through cracks in the woodwork to watch dancers in the sleazier dance halls.

Tired of the police bringing him home at all hours, his parents decided on a change. The day after his sixteenth birthday, his mother had packed his belongings, and waved goodbye when his father placed him on a train north. He hadn't seen them, or any of his family, since.

The letter from his oldest sister had been a surprise. Cole didn't know how she'd found him, and after reading the contents of the letter, he no longer cared.

Hearing the legs of a chair scrape across the scarred wood floor, Cole glanced up to see Gabe joining him. Neither spoke as the sheriff ordered a whiskey. Stretching out his long legs, he crossed them at the ankles, and waited. It was a tactic Gabe had used often.

"I received a letter from my oldest sister. She's asking me to come home to New York." Reaching into a pocket, Cole dragged out the letter, handing it to his boss.

Gabe read the contents twice before handing it back. "Do you believe what she says is true?"

"Could be. I don't know for certain." Blowing out a slow breath, he slid the letter back into the pocket.

"When are you leaving?"

"Tomorrow. I shouldn't be gone more than a month."

"Take as much time as you need, Cole. Your job will be waiting when you get back." Gabe downed his whiskey and stood, holding out his hand.

Cole rose, gripping the outstretched hand. "Thanks, Gabe. I will be back."

"I'm counting on it."

"I can't believe there's no sign of Kev. We've been searching for two days, and there have been no tracks, nothing to indicate my brother was ever out here." Vince held the reins of his horse while walking the area around him.

He felt as if his world were falling apart. Kev, his best friend and older brother, had vanished.

"We'll keep looking, Vince," Thane said. "We aren't going to give up."

"I appreciate it, but we both know Bram needs us at the ranch." For a moment, Vince thought he'd humiliate himself by letting a tear fall.

"He isn't dead. If he were, we would've found some signs. Clothing, his horse, tack, his weapons." Thane didn't mention what they were both thinking. The remains of a body. "I believe it's because he's still alive. Maybe injured, or hiding, but alive. We'll ride back and talk to Bram. And we'll continue searching."

A crack of thunder drew their attention to the north, the direction of the MacLaren ranch. "We'd better get going, Vince."

"Right." Swinging into the saddle, he took another glance around before reining his horse north.

As much as he might want to, Thane didn't rush the ride home. Finding Kevin took priority over everything else. He and Vince had become family over their time at the ranch.

The MacLarens had never built a bunkhouse, resulting in the brothers sharing a bedroom in the ranch house. Everyone took meals together, shared the chores, and worked side by side when moving cattle. When Bram and Thane worked with horses at the Pelletier ranch, Redemption's Edge, they trusted Kevin and Vince to keep the MacLaren place operating.

Thane simply couldn't believe Kevin was gone. Injured, disoriented perhaps. Maybe his horse ran off, leaving him to find his way back to the ranch. From their current location, it would take at least five days to reach the ranch by foot.

What he didn't want to consider was Kevin being attacked by renegade Crow. The band had plagued the land between Big Pine and Splendor for years. They'd recently begun raiding ranches south of the trail between the two towns. He and Bram kept expecting them to attack their ranch. So far, they'd left it alone.

But a lone traveler, such as Kevin, would be easy prey. His rifle, six-shooter, and horse would interest them more.

Glancing to his side, he watched Vince. He kept his gaze moving back and forth across the trail and into the brush on either side. Thane wondered if he'd thought of the Crow renegades, considered they may have taken Kevin.

"Thane, if the Crow found Kev, where would they take him?"

"I don't know. They have a village in the hills north of the trail between Splendor and Big Pine. It's hard to find, and easy for them to defend. Not even the commandant at Fort Connall sends soldiers in there."

"You're saying if they did take him, there's little chance of getting him back."

"What I believe is the Crow didn't find Kev. Something else is keeping him from us. He could be injured, maybe his horse ran away, he's lost, or holed up somewhere. What's important to remember is we are not going to give up."

"What do you think Bram will say?"

"The same as me. No matter what has to be done at the ranch, we will continue the search. I'm going to ride into town tomorrow to see if the sheriff will organize a search party. It's too large an area for two or three men."

Thane wouldn't share his fear they might never find Kevin.

Chapter Twelve

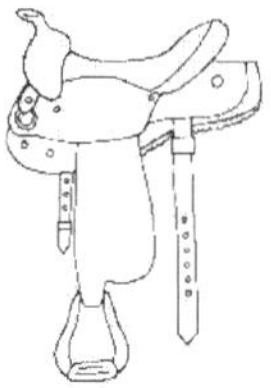

Cole stared up the street toward Martha's house. The stagecoach heading to Big Pine would be arriving in Splendor soon. After a thirty minute stop, the stage would be on its way out of town, sticking to the long established schedule.

Making a quick decision, he took purposeful steps toward her house. Cole changed his mind twice before stopping at the base of her porch. A minute passed before he bounded up the steps, and knocked.

He'd said goodbye to Martha yesterday. To his relief, good upbringing had stopped her from asking why he was leaving or when he'd return.

Cole knew the way he'd acted the last few months had been unfair to her. But nothing had been the same since he'd received the letter.

Reading the contents, his plans to court Martha slipped away. Until he took care of the business detailed in his sister's letter, he couldn't commit to any woman. Still, he didn't want to leave before seeing her one more time.

The door opened on a low groan. "Cole? I thought you'd already left."

Removing his hat, he took a step toward her. "I'll be leaving real soon. I just wanted to say goodbye, Martha."

His words made it sound so final. "You did that yesterday. My understanding was you don't know if you'll ever return to Splendor." She wrapped both arms around her waist.

"There is a chance I won't be able to come back."

Her brows furrowed. "You make it seem as if someone else controls your future."

Fingering the brim of his hat, Cole felt the pressure to explain everything to Martha. Yet he couldn't. Not until he confirmed if what his sister had written was true or just a way to get him back home.

"In a sense, what happens isn't within my control." Hearing the bell at the stagecoach station ring twice, Cole felt his life being torn in two. He had five minutes to get back to the station or miss the stage.

"If it's all right, I'll write you."

One shoulder lifted in a partial shrug. "All right, Cole."

Stepping closer, he bent, brushing a chaste kiss across her cheek. "Take care of yourself, Martha."

Throat thick, she gave an almost imperceptible nod as he turned to dash up the street.

"Good morning, Thane. What brings you to town?" Gabe stood, holding out his hand to grip Thane's outstretched one.

"Do you have a few minutes to talk?"

"Sit down. I have whatever time you need."

Thane explained about Kevin, and what he hoped Gabe could provide. "Can you help us?"

"You say it has been about three days since Kevin disappeared?"

"Almost four."

"You found no tracks, no sign of him during two days of searching?"

Thane let out a strained breath. "Nothing at all. We'll understand if you think another search would be a waste of time."

Shoving back his chair, Gabe stood. "Not at all. We'll need to move quickly. The first person we'll get to help is Noah Brandt. I can spare four deputies." Grabbing his hat, he motioned for Thane to follow him. "I guarantee all the deputies will want to help. We want men who are trackers. Cash Coulter and Beau Davis would be my first choices. I'll send someone out to the Pelletier ranch. You know Travis Dixon?"

"I do."

"One of the best trackers for a hundred miles. I'm hoping Dax and Luke allow him to ride with us." His steps were rushed as he headed toward the saddle and tack shop Noah owned. "We'll get enough men to start a search tomorrow morning."

"Can't ask for more, Gabe."

"Head back home, Thane. Let me organize the search. We'll meet you at your ranch an hour after sunrise tomorrow."

"Are you sure you don't need me here?"

Gabe smiled. "This is part of my job. Yours is at the ranch. The men and I will see you tomorrow morning."

"If you're sure?"

"I am. And do not head out on another search of your own. We're going to start again tomorrow, and that includes you and Vince."

"This is the best opportunity we're going to get, Hugo." Everett stuffed a few clothes into his saddlebags. "I've ordered food from the kitchen for both of us. It will be almost too easy."

Hugo leaned a shoulder against the door, arms crossed. "It's not a good idea, Ev. Ezra has already made a deal with Pinkerton to use one of their agents. The man is on his way. Us taking Sophrona could ruin Ezra's plans. I don't know about you, but I need this job."

"You're making too much of this. We join the search, and when the men leave the MacLaren ranch, we take Sophrona. We'll have her back in San Francisco before the Pinkerton man arrives in Splendor."

"I don't like it. We agreed to no longer worry about Sophrona and let the agent arrest her. All we have to do is wait, then accompany him and Sophrona back to San Francisco. That's what I intend to do."

Everett turned his back on Hugo. When he whirled back around, he held a .44 in his hand, pointed at his partner's chest.

"You're going with me."

"Are you out of your mind, Ev?"

"I'm tired of Ezra changing the rules. And I hate this town. It's time to end this and get the girl." He continued to train the gun on Hugo.

"So you're going to shoot me if I refuse to go with you? What will you tell Ezra if you do make it back to San Francisco?"

"One of the men in the search party thought you were a threat and shot you. If you believe Ezra will care, then you don't know the man. We're nothing to him. I doubt he'd ask a single question about your death."

Jaw clenched, Hugo considered his limited options. He didn't appreciate being threatened, yet Everett was just crazy enough to pull the trigger.

"How would you explain my dead body in your hotel room?"

"Easy. You pulled a gun on me. I fired first. You'll be dead, so no one to dispute my claim."

As ridiculous as it sounded, Hugo knew Everett had a good chance of getting away with murder.

"Fine. I'll go along with your plan. But don't forget I warned you Ezra isn't going to appreciate us interfering in his plans. He's obligated to pay Pinkerton for the agent, even if we bring him Sophrona."

Putting away the gun, Everett threw back his head and laughed. "Ezra's got so much money he won't waste a thought on paying for the agent. Don't forget, marrying the girl will make him one of the wealthiest men in California. The man's ambition will carry him to the state capitol, and we'll be right there with him."

Hugo wasn't so certain about Ezra's wealth or his plans to be governor. Right now, he'd go along with Everett. If it all went sour, he'd eliminate Everett and head back east, where he'd never again have to deal with backward frontier towns.

MacLaren Ranch

"I don't like the idea of you leaving Selina, Sadie, and the babies, Bram. Vince and I will join Gabe and his men for the search while you take care of the ranch."

Thane walked to the window in the room used as an office, looking out into the darkening sky. "Did you hear me, big brother?"

"Aye."

"What are you thinking?"

"About tomorrow? I don't have an answer for you. Not yet." Bram made notations in the journal used for ranch income and expenditures. “It will depend on how many men ride out with Gabe.”

“Have you said anything to Selina?”

“Nae. She’d say the same as you.”

Thane chuckled. “Smart lass.”

Bram didn’t join in the humor. “What if those men return? They’ll be able to overpower the women and take Sadie.”

“What are you two so serious about?” Cradling Connor in her arms, she sat down on one of two well-worn upholstered chairs. A moment later, Sadie joined them, holding Audrey.

“Gabe Evans is organizing a group to search for Kevin. They’ll be here early tomorrow morning.”

“You have to go with them, Bram.” Selina’s quick response surprised the men. “Were you debating whether you should stay here with us?” She motioned toward Sadie.

“It’ll depend on how many men Gabe brings with him, lass.” Bram finished entering information in the journal, sliding it into a drawer.

“I’m surprised those men haven’t returned.” Thane knelt by Sadie’s chair, trailing a finger along Audrey’s cheek. “No matter the number of men, you should stay, Bram.”

“I’ll decide in the morning.” Walking around the desk, he lifted his son from Selina’s arms. “We’ve not sent word to the Pelletiers about Audrey and Connor. The women will want to visit.”

"Gabe mentioned including Travis in the search party. He's an expert tracker. If the women don't know about Audrey and Connor, he'll take word back to the Pelletiers." Straightening, Thane walked to the window.

"What's wrong, Thane?"

He turned back toward Sadie. "Nothing. Let's go outside for a bit." Holding out his hand, he helped her out of the chair.

"I'll take Audrey," Selina said, flashing a knowing look at Thane. She'd seen the way the two watched each other since Thane had returned. "Take some pie out to Vince. He didn't eat much supper."

"Good idea." Sadie hurried down the stairs with Thane right behind her. "Should we take some of the stew with us?"

"We'll take a large piece of pie for now." He stood beside her, feeling a tug in his chest. Wondering what it was about the woman who'd captured his attention, Thane took a step away. The pressure in his chest didn't ease.

Holding the plate with a slice of pie, Sadie stayed close to his side, using the lantern to guide their way to the barn. Inside, Vince mucked clean stalls, tossed items aside before retrieving them, muttering to himself the entire time.

"Hey, Vince." She walked to him, offering him the plate. "We thought you might be ready for this."

Fisted hands on his hips, he stared at the ground before reaching out. "Thank you. I am a little hungry." Taking a bite, he hummed with pleasure. "This is real good. Did you make it?"

A laugh burst from her throat. "Not me. Selina made it while I watched the twins."

"Do you cook?" Thane blanched, not meaning to ask the question.

"Not really. I've never had to learn. Selina has promised to teach me."

"Does that mean you're staying in Splendor?" Vince asked around a mouthful of pie.

She shot a look at Thane. "I don't believe I'll have that choice."

"We aren't going to let those men from California take you away. Right, Thane?"

"No one is going to take her anywhere she doesn't want to go. She just has to trust us." A grin tipped up the corners of his mouth. "There's something I want to show Sadie. Will you be out here long, Vince?"

"I'll wait until you get back. We can walk to the house together." His meaning was clear. They had to remain watchful.

The three of them together would always be better than one or two.

Chapter Thirteen

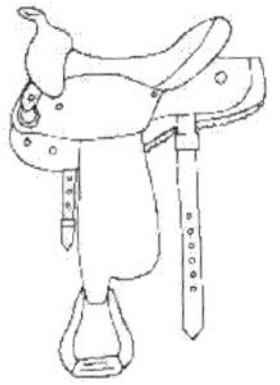

"We'll all ride to the location Vince last saw Kevin. Three groups will ride from there to search." Gabe's gaze swept the men who'd volunteered. Deputies Cash Coulter, Beau Davis, Hawke DeBell, and Hex Boudreaux, Travis Dixon from Redemption's Edge ranch, Noah Brandt, plus Thane, and Vince. Including Gabe, nine men.

The three newest deputies, Morgan, Jonas, and Tucker were eager to help. With Cole gone, Gabe needed them in town. Dax and Luke Pelletier had offered more men, but spring round-up would leave them short those men.

Thane placed a hand on Sadie's shoulder, wishing he could stay behind to protect them. "Bram will make sure you're safe."

Leaning into him, she raised her head to meet his gaze. "I hope you find Kev."

"We have to." He wasn't sure what inspired his next move, but he bent to brush a kiss across her forehead. "Be safe, Sadie. I'll be back soon." Grabbing the reins of his horse, he swung into the saddle.

Surprise coursed through her at his act of affection. Feeling her face heat, she wondered what it meant. Probably nothing, yet she found herself hoping it did.

"Questions?" When no one responded, Gabe nodded at Vince, who took the lead.

Bram stood on the back stoop, his hands clutching the handrail. He'd been torn between going with the men or staying with his wife and twin newborns. Knowing the odds the two men who'd threatened Sadie would most likely return, there wasn't a choice. Protecting his family came first.

"What should we do now, Bram?" Selina cradled Connor in her arms.

Guiding her back inside, where Sadie sat at the kitchen table with Audrey, he pulled out a chair. Once she was comfortable, he walked to the window.

"My instincts tell me the men after Sadie are out there watching us. We need to prepare for them coming after her."

"If you loan me a horse, I'll ride to town."

Turning around, he rested his hip against the counter. "You won't get a hundred yards before they capture you, Sadie. You'll be safer here with us."

Locking the back door, he walked through the house, doing the same with the side and front doors. Confirming all except the second story windows were closed, he grabbed the shotgun, rifle, and two six-shooters left behind.

He loaded each one, placing them next to windows in the upstairs bedrooms. Retrieving his .44 from its spot on the dresser, he headed downstairs.

The women hadn't moved. "I think it would be best if you stay upstairs with the twins. I've placed guns by the windows."

"Where will you be, Bram?" Selina shoved back her chair, forcing herself to stand. "You aren't going outside, are you?"

"Not for a while. We took care of the chores before Gabe arrived with his men. I doubt the men after Sadie care anything about the livestock."

"Well, they're horrible for going after a woman. What kind of men do that?" Selina shifted to look at Sadie.

"Men who are paid well by someone who's more evil than them," Sadie answered in a flat voice. "Where is the safest place for the babies if Wardell and Platt come after me?"

Selina smiled down at Connor. "Upstairs with us. There are two of them and three of us. They have no idea what awaits them if they're foolish enough to try and take you."

"Go on and head upstairs." Bram whirled around to peer out the window at the sound of approaching horses. "Sadie. Are these the men?"

Rushing forward, she stared out, her body going rigid. "Yes."

"Upstairs with you. Keep the babes away from the windows." Drawing his .44 from its holster, he checked the chamber one more time.

The sound of the women's shoes on the stairs brought him scant relief. He didn't want to kill either of the men who reined their horses to a stop several feet from the back door. If they threatened the women and his children, Bram wouldn't hesitate putting bullets in one or both.

Watching through the window, he aimed his .44 at the taller of the two when they drew their six-shooters.

"I wouldn't recommend coming any closer, lads." His shouted warning stopped their approach.

"We aren't looking for trouble," the taller one shouted back.

"If that's true, holster your guns and state your business."

Sliding their weapons away, the shorter man spoke for the first time. "We've come to get Sophrona Thompson. She's wanted in San Francisco for stealing a large sum of money from her fiancé."

"Do you have proof?"

The two men looked at each other, then back at where Bram appeared in the open window. "We can get it."

"Proof the sheriff will accept," Bram added. "If it isn't official, don't bother coming back."

The men nodded before remounting and reining their horses toward town. In a move Bram almost missed, the two pulled their guns, whirled around to aim them at the kitchen window. Before they could fire, a shot rang out, followed by the boom of a shotgun.

Wardell and Platt had no time to react before the shock gave way to lethal pain. A moment later, their lifeless bodies tumbled to the ground.

Splendor Home for Orphans

Martha van Plew used the last of the water in her bucket to wipe down the kitchen counter. She, Ruth Paige, and three other church women had been working for several days to prepare the house for the arrival of several orphans from Big Pine.

They'd started with an eight-bedroom house, which had sat vacant for months after the three families moved south. Cleaning until their hands were raw, the finished result was a sparkling home for the new occupants. What had once been four orphans had grown to six, still well under the home's capacity.

There were two outhouses, which, courtesy of Noah Brandt, were soon to be replaced by indoor water closets. The kitchen had been built twice as large as those in most houses, with two stoves, and room for a third. The dining room could seat eighteen at one table, with an additional ten at another.

Martha had sent a letter to her mother, exclaiming the house was larger than the more modest mansions in Boston. She loved what it represented. Children without a family would now have a safe place to live, three meals, and a warm bed.

The women still faced one major hurdle. They hadn't found the perfect person to run the school.

A committee of five hadn't found a single person willing to manage the home. Martha understood the lack of prospects.

Providing a structured schedule while overseeing the children's behavior was a start. Teaching at different age levels, cooking, cleaning, laundry, and acting as a surrogate parent were equally important.

Ruth had reminded Martha the students would be expected to help with all the chores, which would lessen the burden somewhat. With the children arriving in a few days, they were under pressure to hire someone soon.

"Have you given any thought to taking the position until we find the right person, Martha?" Ruth sipped coffee in the huge kitchen of the home.

They were alone, the other women having left after storing the cleaning supplies. "I'm not a teacher, Ruth, and I'm just learning to cook. Laundry and cleaning aren't an issue. Shopping is fine as long as someone tells me what and how much to buy." Sighing, she shook her head. "Perhaps another woman would share the job with me until the right person is found."

"We can seek someone to share the work with you." Ruth drummed fingers on the table as she worried her lower lip with her teeth. "I could speak with Reverend Paige about making an announcement of our need on Sunday." She spoke of her husband, feeling confident he'd help them get the word out.

"I don't know any of them well, but what about one of Rachel Pelletier's friends who came to Splendor?"

Ruth's eyes lit with excitement. "Amelia Newhall is a teacher by training, but works at the Eagle's Nest. She's an assistant cook and works with May Covington. The last I talked to her, Amelia told me she loved working as a cook. She could be perfect. I'll talk to her tomorrow."

"Honestly, I can't see how one person can do everything required."

"I believe you're right, Martha. A married couple runs the home in Big Pine, plus they have two others who help with cleaning, laundry, and food preparation. I'm going to speak with Rose Keenan, another of Rachel Pelletier's friends who traveled from New York. She's the teacher in Splendor. She and Amelia are roommates."

Checking her pendant watch, Ruth rose. "I have to get back to the church. Are you ready to leave?"

"I am."

The ride back in Ruth's buggy took little time. The house had been built half a mile south of town. To some, it seemed a good distance. The buggy covered the distance in fifteen minutes. A horse would take less than half the time.

The entire ride, Martha thought of Cole, wondering where he was and when he'd be back. She couldn't let herself believe he'd never return. If he did decide to build a life somewhere else, would he send her a telegram or letter?

They'd made no promises, which meant she could be waiting for a man with no intention of coming back. The thought lay heavy on her heart.

New York City

Cole sat in the huge living room of his childhood home, wondering why anyone would want to live in such a cold, impersonal place. He'd never felt any sense of comfort or love in the cavernous structure.

As the youngest of eight, he'd been invisible to both parents and most of his siblings. The exception was his oldest sister, Camilla. She'd always been kind to him, inserting herself between him and their parents when he required protection.

Those attempts to shield him from the severe hand of their father was the reason he'd traveled across country. If the plea had come from anyone else in the family, he'd still be in Splendor, courting Martha van Plew.

"Columbus." His sister's breathy voice came from behind him.

Standing, a smile grew at the sight of her. Tall for a woman, Camilla's slender form glided toward him, stopping inches away. Placing her hands on his shoulders, she kissed his left cheek, then his right before stepping back.

"You're so much taller than I remember, Columbus."

"It's been a long time, Camilla. I was sixteen when Father sent me away." Avoiding any discussion of that painful period, he reached out, taking her hands in his. "You are a beautiful sight."

Laughing, she motioned to the chairs. "Sit down. Edgar will be in with refreshments." She lowered her voice. "We're the only ones in the house today, so we'll be able to talk without fear of our conversation reaching the wrong ears."

Waiting for her to take a seat, he lowered himself back into the large chair. He tapped his pocket. "Your letter was more than intriguing. First, though, how did you find me?"

"Oh, that. You don't think Father would sit back wondering where you'd gone off to, do you?"

"I never gave it a moment's thought."

"Spoken like the impulsive, impish boy of years ago." She quieted when Edgar set down the tray, pouring tea into two cups.

Cole cocked a brow. "Would you have any whiskey, Edgar?"

"Why yes, we do, sir." As tall and rigid as Cole remembered, he stepped to an ornate table, picking up a bottle. "Your father's best, sir."

When Edgar stoked the fire in the large fireplace and left, Cole lifted his glass in a toast. "To seeing my favorite sister."

"And to you. May you always be a scamp."

"Are you ready to enlighten me as to why I'm here, or will you subject me to eating some of, well...whatever food is on the tray before we talk?"

"I won't make you wait. There are actually two reasons for my letter." Setting her teacup down, she leaned forward. "Father is quite ill. He's not expected to last another month."

He tried to summon the proper despair, falling far short. "I'm sorry, Cam. I know how much you love him."

"Yes, I do. However, I've grown quite used to his long illness. Mother is the one I worry about. She has depended on Father her entire life. Since they were children. I'm afraid she won't last long after he's gone."

He offered a solemn nod. "What can I do?"

"Nothing really. You being here is quite wonderful. I'd love to have a supper with all of our family while you're here."

Holding up his hands, he shook his head. "Let's not move too fast. You mentioned two reasons why I'm here. What is the second?"

Sighing, she removed a slip of paper from a pocket in her skirt. "A woman approached me months ago, asking me to give you this." She held it out.

Taking it, Cole unfolded the paper, reading the contents. When finished, comprehension caused his shoulders to slump. "I often wondered..."

Chapter Fourteen

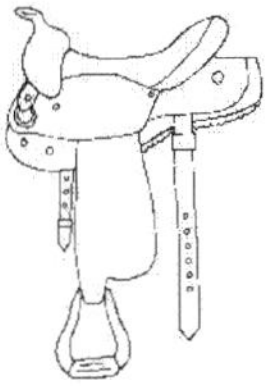

MacLaren Ranch

"Two days and no sign of Kevin. Nothing at all." Frustration laced Gabe's voice. "I don't believe more men would've found anything."

Bram looked past Gabe toward where Thane stood with Vince, a hand on their friend's shoulder. "Why is that?"

"I think he's alive. Possibly lost. Maybe hiding from whatever threatens him. If something had happened to him, we would've found evidence. Do you understand what I'm saying, Bram?"

"Aye. The lad is alive, but we don't know where. What about the renegade band of Crow?"

"That's possible, but I don't believe they have him." Gabe ran a hand down his face. "We've had several people go missing since I became sheriff. There were always signs. Pieces of clothing, signs of a struggle. Blood."

"It was raining when he disappeared. Tracks could've washed away."

"Maybe. Instinct tells me Kev made it through the storm. He disappeared afterward."

"We could keep searching. If he is alive, he'll show up somewhere." Bram didn't want to tell Vince there was no hope.

"That's your decision, Bram. I hate to quit, but I've got to get my men back to town. Travis has already ridden on to Redemption's Edge. I'm sorry we didn't find him."

"Not your fault, Gabe. I know you and your men did all you could. Thank you for trying."

"I'd better get going."

Bram glanced around, confirming no one else could hear them. "There is something else. Something you must see."

Motioning for Gabe to follow him, Bram walked around the side of the house. He stopped next to a large piece of canvas.

"Tell me that's not what I think it is."

Bending down, Bram pulled back a corner to reveal two bodies. "Everett Wardell and Hugo Platt."

Shoving back his hat, Gabe blew out a breath. "Guess we should go inside so you can explain what happened. I also expect coffee. Lots of coffee."

New York City

"I'm sorry, Columbus. I never should've sent for you." Camilla wrung her hands, distraught at the resignation on his face. Reaching forward, she plucked the paper from his hand. “We’ll burn it. Never speak of it again.”

Cole didn’t respond right away. Rubbing his eyes with the palms of his hands, he raised his head to meet her expectant gaze.

“No. The others deserve to know.”

“They don’t deserve any such thing.” Rising, she walked toward the fireplace.

“That won’t change the truth, Cam.”

“We don’t know if it’s true or not.” She held the paper up. “This may be a lie. I should’ve dug deeper before writing to you.” Folding the letter, she tucked it back into the pocket of her skirt. “I’ll hire a detective to sort this out. Perhaps Pinkerton.”

Joining her, Cole placed a hand on her shoulder. “It’s all right, Camilla. I’ve suspected as much for a long time.”

“What?”

“Father and Mother said things when they believed none of us were around.”

Camilla raised a brow. “But you were?”

“I was. Eavesdropping was quite fun when I was young. They’d talk about their children. They often spoke about me. Sometim tey’d argue. Now it makes sense.”

“What did they say?”

“It’s been a long time.”

“Meaning you never heard them confirm anything alleged in the letter. Children have incredible imaginations.”

"True. All I can say right now is I'm not surprised at what the letter says."

"You may have heard bits and pieces of a conversation. Over the years, the fragments transformed into something else. By the time you were older, they'd transformed into an entirely different meaning."

"Ah, Cam. You've always had a soft spot for me."

A warm smile appeared. "That doesn't mean the letter isn't full of falsehoods. All this makes me more determined to hire an investigator to discover the truth."

Cole didn't respond. He'd suspected the truth for years. Though he'd hoped he was wrong. If the contents of the letter were accurate, his life had been a lie.

"You have to stay long enough to visit with Father and Mother, and to determine if the letter is genuine."

"I have a job in Montana. One I'm good at."

"You'd be good at anything." She raised a hand when he opened his mouth to respond. "I respect you have a life out west. I'm only asking for a little time before you go back."

"How little?"

"Two, maybe three weeks. It shouldn't take long to ascertain the accuracy of the letter."

"One week is as long as I can stay."

"Then I must start today."

"There's no need to hire someone, Cam. The easiest way to discover the truth is to ask Father and Mother."

"The doctor won't allow us to upset Father. I'm certain what we want to know will cause him distress."

"Perhaps if I spoke to him alone. It would take less than a minute to answer the only question I have."

Camilla knew he was right. The issue wasn't so much the question he asked or the answer. Either way, their father would be all right, and life would remain the same within the Santori family.

The real problem had nothing to do with the letter. It was a predicament Cole knew nothing about. A life-changing situation which couldn't be resolved with a simple question and answer.

MacLaren Ranch

"Come outside with me, Sadie." Thane held out his hand, pleased when she threaded her fingers with his.

The deaths of Wardell and Platt meant the threat to Sadie had ended. At least the threat from the two gunslingers. Whatever Ezra planned next would take time to organize.

Gabe had sent a telegram to San Francisco, notifying him of the deaths. The sheriff received no response.

"It's hard for me to accept I shot a man." Sadie didn't look at him as they walked toward the corral. "Of course, Selina may have shot both of them."

"She doesn't think so. Selina told Gabe she aimed at Wardell and fired. Before she could aim again, Platt had fallen from his horse. You hit what you aimed for, Sadie." He tightened his hold on her hand. "Try not to dwell on it."

"It's just there, Thane. Squeezing the trigger, then Platt falling to the ground. It goes around and around in my head. The only time it's not there is when I'm asleep. I hate it." Her voice broke on the last.

Letting go of her hand, he stopped, wrapping her in his arms. When she wrapped hers around him, he rested his chin on the top of her head.

"It will get easier, sweetheart. What you have to remember is you shot Platt to protect me and Bram. Their deaths were justified."

"The sheriff said the same." She leaned back, looking up at him. "Ezra won't take their deaths well. I'd be surprised if he doesn't send other men to take their places. I'm so tired of him trying to run my life."

Cupping her face in his hands, he met her gaze. "You're safe here with us. We aren't going to let anything happen to you."

"I can't stay here forever."

"Sure you can." He brushed a soft kiss across her lips. "I hope you'll consider staying forever."

Sadie sat on her bed long into the night, thinking about Thane's request she stay. The comment had surprised her into silence. She'd waited for him to say more, but he'd slipped his hand back in hers, resuming their walk.

Now she couldn't sleep. One positive outcome of Thane's comment was she hadn't thought too much about the shooting. Or Ezra.

Stretching out under the covers, she clasped her hands together on her stomach, staring at the ceiling. What would Ezra do once he heard about his two henchmen?

Maybe nothing. There was a chance, although slim, he'd forget about her, find another woman to fulfill his dream of becoming governor. Knowing her parents, they would still donate to his campaign.

Being friends with Ezra Crockett had always meant more to them than building a relationship with their daughter. They didn't seem to care what Sadie thought of them. Doing as her father ordered was what made him, and her mother, happy.

Happiness for Sadie had always been elusive. She remembered being happy when young. There'd been no expectations other than acting appropriately, eating all her food, and going to bed when asked. At sixteen, it all changed.

Sadie had been introduced to Ezra by her parents at a social event. His plans to marry her had begun that night, as did the way she was treated at home.

Her parents hired a tutor to increase her knowledge in numbers, writing, and language. They'd also brought in a piano teacher and dance instructor. Instead of spending hours talking about boys with her girlfriends, Sadie found herself in a closed room with one of the people trying to improve her skills.

Staring at the ceiling, a smile curved her lips. She wondered what her parents and Ezra would think of her now, living on a ranch in Montana. And proficient enough with a shotgun to kill a man. This time, when she thought of Hugo Platt lying on the ground, she didn't flinch.

Sadie reminded herself if she hadn't shot him, he would've shot Thane or Bram. Possibly Selina or her, if he'd raised his gaze to spot them in the upstairs window. It had turned out to be a bad day for him and Everett Wardell.

A cold chill ran through her body. Deep down, she knew this wasn't the end of her trials. Ezra wouldn't take the loss calmly and forget about her. He'd come up with another plan to spirit her away from Splendor.

It was a matter of when, and what kind of devil he'd send next.

Chapter Fifteen

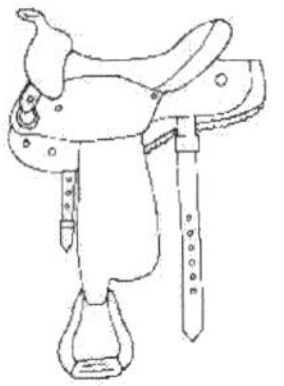

An earsplitting cry woke Sadie from what had been a dream. A good one where she and Thane walked along a creek, picking berries.

Blinking, she stretched as another cry came from down the hall. *The babies.*

Throwing off the covers, she jumped out of bed. Dressing without thought, she ran a brush through her hair before rushing toward the unhappy babes.

Entering Selina's bedroom, Sadie was relieved to find Bram nowhere in sight. Selina nursed one of the babies while the other fussed in its bed. Bending down, Sadie lifted Connor, cradling him against her chest.

Selina's gaze shifted from Audrey to her son. "He's hungry. She's almost finished."

Sadie paced around the room, rocking Connor to calm him while Audrey drank her fill. Hearing a soft knock, she opened the door, not surprised to see Thane.

"Good morning."

"Morning, Sadie. Bram's fixing breakfast and wants to know if you two can join us and Vince."

"How is Vince?" Sadie asked. Her heart ached for him.

"Not too good. He's been in the barn and working the horses for a couple hours already. Maybe keeping busy helps."

Sadie nodded. "Makes sense. Tell Bram we'll be down in a little bit. This big boy still has to eat." She smiled down at Connor.

When they did join Thane and Bram, Vince wasn't at the table. Sadie offered to find him, but Bram shook his head.

"Let the lad be, lass. He'll come inside when he's ready."

Selina pushed around her food, taking a small bite, then setting her fork down. "You said Gabe believes he's alive. Where's his horse, tack, saddlebags? Did he find a place to hide large enough for a horse? Why would he be hiding? There are so many questions."

"And no answers." Vince stood in the doorway, removing his boots. "Is there still any breakfast left?"

"Plenty. Sit down." Bram moved to the counter, filling a plate with bacon, potatoes, and eggs. "Will this be enough?"

Taking the plate, Vince sat down next to Thane. Staring at the food, hunger won out and he dug in. The others resumed eating, the conversation changing.

"We have ten trained horses to deliver to the Pelletiers." Bram shot looks at Thane and Vince. "It will take all three of us to drive them to the ranch."

"When do you want to go?" Thane glanced at Sadie.

"Today. We'll be bringing back seven wild horses." Bram reached out, taking Selina's hand. "We'll be gone no more than six hours."

She read the question in his voice. "We'll be fine."

Sadie nodded in agreement, although a tinge of worry lodged in her stomach. How long would it take for Ezra to send someone else to Splendor?

"I'll do the laundry and start supper while you take care of the twins, Selina."

"I can help. Once they're fed, the babies will sleep for a few hours."

Bram looked at his wife skeptically, keeping his thoughts to himself. "Get our gear ready, lads. We'll leave as soon as we round up the horses."

San Francisco

Ezra crushed the telegram in his hand, his face heating in anger. According to the sheriff in the small Montana settlement, Wardell and Platt were dead in a justified shooting.

The sheriff hadn't mentioned who'd shot them or the circumstances. It didn't matter. They were dead and wouldn't be returning to San Francisco. Their deaths forced him to take time from his already busy schedule to hire replacements.

"This city has hundreds of men willing to do my business," he muttered under his breath.

More than any town Ezra could think of, San Francisco welcomed those with dubious backgrounds and unsavory morals.

Tossing the crumpled paper across the room, he scribbled two messages before walking to the door of his office. "Nelson!"

A short, rotund man with thinning hair and a double chin appeared from a nearby room. "Yes, sir?"

"Give these to one of the beggars outside." He pulled two coins from a pocket. "One coin to deliver them to the telegraph office. The second when they return here with confirmation the messages have been sent. Questions?"

"No, sir." Taking the coins and papers, he whirled around, racing down the steps at a speed most would think impossible for a man of his girth.

Returning to his desk, he completed entering numbers in the second set of ledgers the recently deceased Malcom Sloan had accused him of using. Before locking them in the safe at the back of a closet, he poured himself a whiskey, toasting Sloan.

It still amazed him how no one suspected he'd been the one to kill the well-liked businessman. Even the police believed Malcom had been shot by street hooligans. Everyone knew the perils of walking the city's streets at night. His dead partner had simply ignored the risks and paid for his mistake.

Dropping onto a sofa, his mind wandered to Sophrona. Such a foolish child, thinking she could run away without consequence. He'd already told her parents what would happen if she didn't return. Her father had moaned in fear while her mother had raged at Ezra. Of the two, he much preferred the woman's reaction to his threats.

Though he found humor in their responses, his threats were quite real. If Sophrona didn't return, her father would disappear, then her mother. The right men could carry out his orders without any evidence leading back to Ezra.

The thought reminded him of the need to hire men to replace Wardell and Platt. Tossing back a second whiskey, he donned his coat and hat.

It was time to visit his friend near the docks. She knew everyone, including who might be looking for work, and if they were the kind of men Ezra would hire. One short trip, and within hours, two men would be on their way to Splendor.

New York City

Cole's shoulders slumped as he leaned forward, kissing his sleeping father's forehead before leaving the older man's bedroom. He'd asked his father one question. After several uncomfortable minutes, Cole received a surprising answer.

Leaving the opulent bedroom where his father would probably take his last breath, he wandered down the hall toward his old bedroom. Opening the door, he sucked in a sharp breath.

He'd thought the room would've been turned into a retreat for guests long ago. Instead, everything was the same as when he'd been sent away at sixteen.

His reading primer lay on the desk where he'd left it. Clothes he'd argued to take but was overruled by his mother, lay strewn across the floor. Outside his closet, a worn baseball rested against a seasoned bat.

Cole's gaze moved up to the expertly made bed. A teddy bear lay against an ornately decorated pillow. Beside it was another toy.

Walking to the bed, he leaned over, grabbing it with shaking hands. His father had given him a bugle. Not a toy, but a real bugle used by Union soldiers during the Civil War. He'd shown Cole how to purse his lips just right to get the most sound.

His throat tightened as he stared at one of his prized possessions. He'd thought his mother would've tossed it, and everything else, out years ago. Why hadn't she?

Sitting on the edge of the bed, he raised the bugle to his lips, blowing lightly. He wanted to do more, knowing the noise would bring all the staff, and Camilla, searching to discover the source. He puffed air through the bugle again before holding it in his lap.

"Columbus. Camilla told me you were here. I didn't believe her." Tall and stately, his mother didn't appear at all the fragile woman his sister had described. She walked to him, arms wide open. "It is so good to see you."

He saw what looked similar to a tear rolling down her face. Cole knew that had to be wrong, as his mother never cried, never shed a tear.

Walking into her arms, his moved around her. He felt, rather than heard, her sob. When they pulled apart, a smile hid any remaining moisture. She cupped his face in her hands and studied him.

"You've grown into a fine man." Kissing his cheek, she stepped away to sit on the edge of the bed. Cole chose to stand.

"You're as beautiful as ever, Mother." It was as if all the years melted away. She hadn't changed at all.

"I'm so anxious to hear about your life out west. You will be staying for a few days." So like his mother. It wasn't a question.

"Yes. But no more than five days. I have a job in Splendor."

"Splendor. What a lovely name. Do the people live up to it?"

"In my opinion, they do. The people are genuine, hardworking, and always willing to help. I believe you would like it. You and Camilla should come for a visit. The St. James hotel and its Eagle's Nest restaurant are excellent. As good as most exclusive hotels in New York."

"Now you're exaggerating."

"Not at all. Do you know the Evans family?"

"The hotel Evans?"

He nodded. “Gabe Evans is the sheriff and one of the hotel owners.”

“Gabriel Evans? Why, we thought he’d died in the war.”

Cole would have to remember to relay this to Gabe. “When his Uncle James died, he left all his holdings to Gabe. He travels to New York at least twice a year to make sure his holdings are being well managed.”

“I don’t know what to say. It sounds so fantastic. Obviously, I must be more careful who I listen to.” Standing, she touched his arm, a soft smile brightening her features. “I can’t tell you how much your visit means to us. Well, I have letters to write before supper. It will be the three of us, so quite casual.” She hesitated a second before stepping into the hall and closing the door.

Cole stood in the same spot, staring at the door. This was not how he remembered his mother. She’d been the true head of the house, making the rules, and doling out punishment, which his father implemented.

This was not the homecoming he’d anticipated. His expectations were colored by a childhood in a family where he never seemed to belong. Most of the time, as the youngest of eight, he was often forgotten. Conversations went on around him about issues he knew nothing about. No one asked his opinion, or tried to draw him out. No one except Camilla.

She was the only reason he’d returned. Anyone else and he’d have declined.

Visiting his father, and learning the truth, had closed one door while opening another. His mother’s welcome had stunned him. Cole couldn't remember any time in his youth where she'd wrapped him in her arms.

All of it had come about because of Camilla. She'd wanted him to visit once more while their parents were still alive.

He didn't know what the next few days would bring. If they were anything like today, Cole had to wonder what other revelations awaited him.

Chapter Sixteen

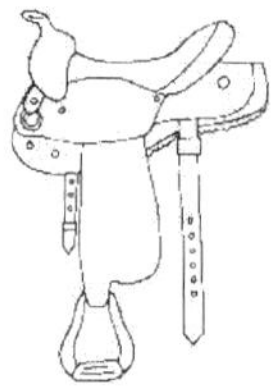

Splendor

Martha could hardly contain her excitement. Amelia Newhall had agreed to become the cook and housekeeper at the home for orphans. Her good friend, Rose Keenan, would be joining her as the home's teacher.

The decision had been difficult for her. With Amelia also leaving her job at the Eagle's Nest kitchen, both women, with teaching experience, would be working with the orphans. The town would have to find someone outside of Splendor to take over in the fall.

Knocking on the door of Ruth Paige's home, Martha fidgeted with the cuff of her blouse. She'd been considering an idea all day. It was time to present it to Ruth.

"Hello, Martha. Please, come inside. I bought lemons in Chinatown and made lemonade. Would you like a glass?"

"I'd love a glass. Let me help you. I have an idea to discuss."

Once settled in Ruth's cozy parlor, Martha took a sip of lemonade, settling against the back of a beautiful needlepoint chair.

"Don't make me wait any longer. I'd love to hear your idea."

"You already know we're leaving the town short a teacher."

"Yes, and I feel terrible about it." Ruth set her glass down. "I'm sure there's a way to fix it, I just don't know what it is."

"Have you thought about taking the orphans to town for schooling?"

Tilting her head, Ruth's forehead furrowed. "I suppose it will depend on how many children are school age and may fit in a wagon. Silas Jenks at the lumberyard donated an old wagon. He fixed it up first, of course. We may be able to fit ten or twelve children, which is more than are arriving from Big Pine."

Ruth's mouth twisted as she thought. Meeting Martha's questioning gaze, she chuckled. "We'll also have to find more chairs and desks for the school. The other issue is what to do when the weather is severe in the winter."

"From what I've heard, if the weather is bad, most of the children stay home. We may find it's not an issue."

Picking up her glass, Ruth sipped lemonade while considering Martha's idea. "Do you foresee Rose continuing as the teacher?"

"It would help out the town if Rose stayed, at least until they found a replacement. Of course, Rose will need to consent to this arrangement. I doubt she'll object."

“I think it’s an excellent idea, Martha. Do you want to speak with Rose? She told me she’d wait to let the town council know about leaving until hearing back from us.”

“I’ll be happy to meet with her.”

“You know, Martha, we should talk about hiring a manager for the home. You’ve volunteered to fill the role until someone suitable is found, which is quite generous of you. However, we all know it isn’t a permanent solution. What are your thoughts?”

Clasping her hands in her lap, Martha considered the question. She loved working with children, was looking forward to the first group arriving from Big Pine. Committing to a permanent position hadn’t been considered.

In truth, she’d been thinking about returning to Boston. With Angela married and Cole’s defection, it made little sense to stay in Splendor. Her parents provided an allowance each month, enough for rent, food, and clothing, but not much else.

Returning to Boston could open the door to greater social opportunities, such as marriage and children. Cole leaving had created a void no other man in Splendor could fill. She loved the town and the people, though social connections were limited. More so with all her friends being married.

There’d been a time when she’d thought Cole would be a good match for her. He loved his job as a deputy, and spoke of building a house on the edge of town. Him leaving had been heartbreaking. It also forced her to evaluate staying in Splendor as a single woman.

"You're right. My overseeing the home isn't a permanent solution. Has anyone spoken to the couple in Big Pine? Perhaps they know of someone suitable."

"I've sent them a letter. They haven't responded yet. We have to consider expanding the search beyond Montana. Perhaps Denver or Kansas City."

"Who would you contact?"

Shrugging, Ruth stood, collecting the empty glasses. "I have no idea. But I'll find out."

New York City

Camilla stared out the large window of the parlor, watching rain pound the enclosed patio. Prior to this, she'd paced back and forth for an hour, wringing her hands, searching for calm, knowing it was impossible. What she had to tell her brother vanished all thoughts of peace.

Cole would be arriving soon from an outing with their mother. In two days, he'd be leaving for Montana. Camilla had put off this discussion longer than practical. Much longer than she should have given the importance of the news she'd be delivering.

The sound of the front door opening, the voices raised in conversation, signaled her procrastination clock had stopped.

"Hello, dear." Their mother swept into the room, the smile on her face bigger than any Camilla had seen in years. She hated what she had to tell Cole could also shake up their mother's world.

"Columbus took me to lunch and the Metropolitan Museum of Art. Can you imagine your brother in a museum?"

"Actually, I can, Mother. He's always been a very inquisitive boy. Now he's a man of many interests." She shot her brother a knowing look, grateful when his mouth tipped into an impish grin. "Did you enjoy the museum, Columbus?"

"I did. The European masters exhibit was magnificent." Bussing a kiss across his sister's cheek, he took a minute to study her. Tension radiated off her, had been for a few days. "Are you feeling unwell, Cam?"

"Perhaps not as good as I could. Would either of you enjoy a refreshment?"

"Nothing for me, dear. I'm going to retire to my room for a time."

"Please, stay," Camilla blurted out before calming her voice. "If you would. There is an important matter I must discuss with Columbus, and I'd prefer you heard what I have to say."

"Sounds ominous, Cam. Perhaps I will pour a whiskey. Would you like one?"

"No, thank you. Maybe afterward..." Her voice trailed off.

"Are you certain you're all right, Cam? You look a little pale."

"Well, I'm not as good as usual."

His brows drew together. "Then you should deliver whatever news you have. You might feel better afterward."

She doubted it, but what choice did she have. "Perhaps you should sit down, Columbus. You, too, Mother."

Both stared at her as if she were a specimen under a microscope, but did as she suggested. Again, she wrung her hands together, then began to pace.

"Camilla, please do sit down yourself. You're making me dizzy."

Stopping, she shot a look at her mother. "You're right, and I apologize. It's just what I have to say won't be easy to hear."

Their mother's eyes brightened. "You're betrothed to the wonderful young man who's been calling on you?"

If only that were it, Camilla thought. "No, Mother. I'm still your only unmarried daughter." Lowering herself into a chair close to Cole, she straightened her shoulders.

"If that isn't it, then I'm going to lay down for a while. Thank you for a wonderful day, Columbus."

"I had a good time, Mother." He walked her to the hall before returning to Camilla.

"Do you recall a woman named Evelyn Anderson?"

His chest squeezed at the memory of the woman he'd once loved. "It's been years. We met when I rode through Kansas City." There was more, though nothing he'd share with Camilla.

"A friend of hers visited here a few months ago. I believe she hoped to find you at home and was quite displeased you weren't around."

"What did she want?"

"Well, she left you something."

A sinking feeling in his stomach ate at his patience. "Left me something?"

Reaching into a pocket of her skirt, she retrieved a folded piece of paper. "She also gave me this. It's for you."

His eyes latched onto the paper as his hands fisted. "What does it say?"

"I think you should read it."

Cole thought of what his father had confirmed soon after he arrived in New York City. After so many years of assuming, his father's admission had been anticlimactic. His mother had been rushed to the hospital when her labor pains grew excruciatingly intense. The baby was stillborn, sending her into an intense depression.

Her deep mood hadn't improved when she returned home. Beyond worried, his father had returned to the hospital. Later that day, he returned home, though he wasn't alone. In his arms was a beautiful baby boy of Italian heritage with olive skin, dark hair, and deep brown eyes. They named him Columbus Marco Dante Santori. Cole Santori.

"Columbus?"

Squeezing his eyes shut for an instant, he opened them to see Camilla holding out the paper. Reaching out, he ot at all sure he was ready for a second ek.

read the contents, his heart pounding hed the end. Hands shaking, he read it efolding it.

d the letter?"

k her head. "I didn't have to. She told me it are you going to do?"

have to look far, Columbus. He's playing in

* * *

valked next to Thane, her arm through his as ed the boardwalk. He'd given a tour of the town, introducing her to many of the shop id citizens.

must love it here."

huckled. "Not sure about love. I have come to ite the town and its people."

y, Thane!"

e couple stopped at the shout from behind them. wing his gaze, Thane recognized Bernie Griggs from legraph office.

"Glad I saw you." Bernie bounded on the bal
feet, looking between Thane and Sadie. "I believe tl
for the lady here. Ma'am, are you Sophrona Thomp

The breath caught in her throat. "Yes, I am."

A broad smile broke out on Bernie's face. "Thi
for you." He waved it in the air before handing i
When she didn't open it, he fixed his gaze on Thane
want me to wait?"

"No, Bernie. If Miss Thompson wants to s
response, we'll come to your office."

"Reckon I'd better get back." He tipped his cap at S
"Ma'am."

"Thank you, Mr....um..."

"Griggs. Bernie Griggs." He hurried down
boardwalk.

"Are you going to open it?"

Worrying her bottom lip, she broke the seal. Her b
tensed when seeing it was from Ezra. The message
short.

"We aren't finished, Sophrona."

Chapter Seventeen

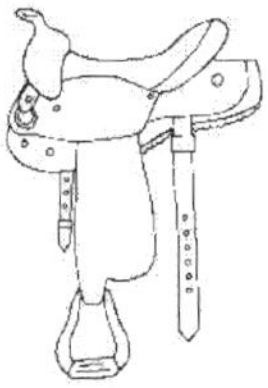

"Start from the beginning, Miss Thompson. I want to hear anything you have to say about Ezra Crockett." Gabe opened the top drawer on his desk, pulling out a telegram.

"I'd prefer it if you'd call me Sadie."

Smiling, he nodded. "Fair enough, Sadie. Tell me everything."

She took her time, explaining about her parent's friendship with Ezra, and his interest in a naïve sixteen-year-old. "He'd proposed when I turned seventeen. I shocked him and my parents by telling him no."

"What did they do when you refused?" Gabe leaned forward, resting his arms on the desk.

"Nothing, at first. For a while, I believed my parents and Ezra respected my decision. Instead, they moved me to his house, thinking I'd grow to like, even love, him if we spent time together."

Anger turned Thane's face red. "You were alone with him?"

"No. They hired a chaperone," she scoffed. "A girl not much older than me, who was a friend of Ezra's. A good friend," she whispered.

"What happened next?"

"Ezra started planning our wedding. He took me to a seamstress. She took measurements and gave me a selection of fabric for a wedding dress. Ezra didn't approve of anything I selected. After that day, he picked everything, reserved the church, sent invitations, and planned the reception. I kept telling him there wasn't going to be a wedding. I had no intention of marrying him. That's when he ordered two men to stay with me at all times. I'd become his prisoner."

Thane placed a hand over hers. "So you ran."

Sadie looked between him and Gabe. "Yes."

Gabe slid the telegram toward her. "Read this."

Reluctantly, she picked up the paper. Her eyes widened, then narrowed as she read. Tossing the paper down, she stood up so fast, the chair would've tipped over if Thane hadn't caught it.

"He's lying. I didn't take a cent from Ezra. The only money I took was what my parents gave me when they moved me into his house."

Stomping to the window, she looked out before whirling around to face Gabe. Taking a breath, she did her best to calm the anger boiling within her.

"Ezra Crockett is an indulgent, arrogant, blight on everything good. He thinks people will believe whatever he says, whether there is merit to his words or not. The telegram is a complete lie."

Rising, Thane put an arm around her shoulders. "Sit down, Sadie. Gabe may have other questions for you."

Expelling a shaky breath, she reclaimed her seat. "Of course. What more do you need to know, Sheriff?"

"Do you recall how much money you brought with you?"

"Two hundred dollars. Most was used for transportation to Splendor. Some for food, though I had little appetite during the trip."

"Where is the remainder of your money?"

"There wasn't much left, Sheriff. It's still in the hotel room, though I'm sure it has already been cleaned."

"Where in the room?"

She glanced at Thane, a mischievous grin tilting her lips upward. "I found a crack in the back of the wardrobe and stuffed it in there."

Chuckling, Gabe leaned back in his chair. "I suppose a telegram to your parents asking them to verify the amount given to you would be fruitless."

One shoulder lifted in a shrug. "They would contact Ezra, and he'd tell them how to respond."

"Will you be staying in Splendor for a while?"

Thane answered for her. "Yes. Sadie will be at our ranch."

She shot him a questioning look, but didn't contradict his answer.

"Good enough. I'm going to the hotel to see if we can find your money. Would you like to accompany me?"

"Yes." Meaning to stand, Sadie placed her hands on the arms of the chair a moment before the door burst open.

"Ah. Sheriff Evans, correct?"

"Yes." Gabe stood.

"Sorry to disturb you. I'm Agent Beardsley from the Pinkerton Agency. I heard you have my fugitive in custody. I've come to escort her back to San Francisco."

Thane sat across the room with Sadie, holding her hand as Paul Beardsley argued he held jurisdiction while Gabe countered a crime hadn't been committed. He challenged the agent to provide proof of the theft Ezra Crockett accused Sadie of committing. Beardsley admitted it was Crockett's word against his fiancée.

"I am not his fiancée, Mr. Beardsley. I turned down his proposal."

"So you stole money and ran away."

"Prove it," she shot back. When he didn't respond, she stood. "Thank you, Sheriff. You've been more than helpful. Good luck to you, Agent Beardsley. You'll need it if you believe anything Ezra tells you." Thane contained a grin as he followed her to the door.

"Now you just wait..." The agent's voice fell off when the jail door slammed closed. He whirled on Gabe. "You're the sheriff. Why did you let her leave?"

"Because the woman didn't create a crime. You've been given bad information. I'm sorry you made a trip for no reason. If it would help, I'll send a telegram to your boss."

"Why would he listen to you?"

"We have several former agents living in Splendor. One works for me. Pinkerton tends to listen to what I have to say."

A big man, tall and broad, Paul lowered himself into a chair, scrubbing a hand down his face.. "You're right. My understanding is Ezra provided no proof of Miss Thompson's theft, other than his word."

Standing, Gabe clasped Paul's shoulder. "I believe we could both use a drink."

New York City

Cole stood at the back door of the spacious kitchen, watching the boy run around the back yard. From Camilla, he'd learned the child, dressed as a little adult, was eight.

His mother, Evelyn Anderson, had been a young widow he'd met in Kansas City. She was the sweetest woman he'd ever met, as was her two-year-old son, Dante. He'd fallen hard, wanted to marry her, but her family had other plans. Six years later, Cole stood at the door of his family's kitchen, watching Dante laugh and run in circles, trying to catch a butterfly.

"He's been living at my house, Columbus," Camilla whispered beside him. "Mother knows nothing about him."

"Dante was two when I last saw him. Cutest little boy I'd ever seen."

"Yes, he is. And smart. I hired a tutor to determine where he was in his studies."

"How far behind is he?"

"Behind? Dante is almost a year ahead of most children his age. Why don't you reintroduce yourself to him?"

"I don't know if I'm ready for this, Cam."

"You haven't been left much choice. If you prefer, I'll go with you." When Cole didn't answer, she stepped outside. "Dante! Come over here, sweetheart. There's someone who wants to see you."

Running toward the house, he smiled at two people in the doorway. "I don't believe that boy walks anywhere. He's always running. You probably already know how much energy he has."

Cole nodded, his throat clogged with emotion. He hadn't known Evelyn and Dante long, a few short months, before her family swept them back to Baltimore. Even so, he'd come to love both of them. Loved them enough to make what seemed an absurd offer. An offer he never dreamed he'd have to fulfill.

Dante came to a sliding stop in front of them. "Aunt Camilla. Did you see the butterfly? It was huuuuge."

"I did. Sweetheart, this is Columbus Santori. You met him when you were much younger."

Dante studied him, his gaze moving upward to settle on Cole's eyes. "I remember. You and Mother were friends."

"Your mother also talked about him as you were growing up."

"Mother said you were a cowboy."

Dropping down to Dante's height, Cole smiled. "I've been a cowboy and a lawman."

Features serious, the young boy's mouth twisted in thought. "We don't have cowboys in New York."

"True, but you have lawmen. I'm a deputy sheriff in Splendor, Montana."

"Mother's dead. So are Grandpa and Grandma." Tears threatened to spill down Dante's face before his small hand swept them away.

"I know. That's why I'm here."

An hour later, after lemonade and cake, Cole had explained his offer to Dante's mother. The boy's first reaction had been to shake his head, saying he'd rather stay with Camilla. When she explained her plans for an extended visit with Dante in Montana, he'd changed his mind, becoming excited about the idea of moving west.

"Will there be Indians?"

"It's possible. There are Blackfoot and Crow tribes not far from Splendor."

"Can we go see them?"

Cole cast an amused look at Camilla. "They aren't the same as a museum or art gallery, Dante. You have to be invited, or have a real good reason for riding to their village."

"Oh." He sat for a moment before perking up. "Will you teach me to use a gun?"

“We’ll talk about it when you’re older.”

“Will I have to go to school?”

“The same as here,” Cole answered. “By the time we get there, school will be out for the summer. I live in town, so there will be plenty to do. I’ll introduce you to boys and girls out on the ranches.”

“They go to the same school?”

“Sure do.”

Dante seemed to consider this before grinning. “When can we leave?”

Chapter Eighteen

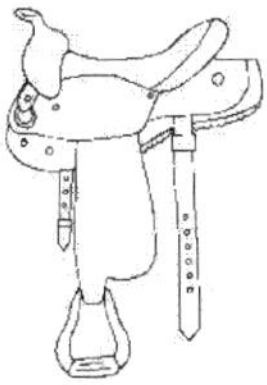

MacLaren Ranch

Sadie's days fell into a comfortable routine, helping care for the twins, cooking, doing laundry, and learning the skills used on a ranch. She'd been surprised to learn Selina could do everything Bram, Thane, and Vince did. Her accomplishments encouraged Sadie, whose experience with horses could be defined as adequate.

Stirring leftover stew on the stove, she bounced Connor on her hip. Audrey played quietly on a blanket placed a few feet away, reaching into the air for something Sadie couldn't see.

A few months ago, she would've told whoever asked she had no desire for children. The answer today would be different. She didn't know when the transition occurred, though she was certain it had something to do with Thane.

"Sadie?"

His voice sent a flash of something she couldn't quite describe. She'd never experienced anything like it when around other men.

"Thane. Do you need something?"

Instead of answering, he stepped behind her, pressing a kiss to her temple. "Selina wants us to bring the twins outside for a bit. It's a beautiful day."

"Warm?"

"You'll need a sweater, and the twins will need a blanket. Bram tossed hay into a pile for us to put them on."

"Let me move the stew so it doesn't burn." By the time she'd slid the pot to the coolest part of the stove, he'd picked up Audrey and the blanket, plus two more blankets already on the table.

She hadn't stepped outside all day, too busy with other chores. "It's spectacular."

"There's no place like it. Not even where I come from."

"Selina said you and Bram are from California. You're from a large family who owns a sizable ranch east of San Francisco."

"You know more than most, Sadie." Bending down, he laid down the blankets, placing Audrey down. Spreading out another blanket, he took Connor from Sadie's arms, laying him beside his sister.

"They're so beautiful."

"So are you, lass." He ran a finger down her cheek, wanting to kiss her. She hadn't discouraged his brief touches of affection. Maybe because they'd never occurred in front of anyone else.

Surprised by his comment, her face flushed. Offering a timid smile, she reached out to run the back of her hand against his. Thane's return grin warmed her.

"There are my babes." Selina rushed her steps to join them. "Have they been good for you, Sadie?"

"Perfect. Bringing them outside was a good idea."

"I've more chores and need to help Bram." Thane cut a look at Sadie before returning to the corral where his brother worked with a young horse.

Sadie didn't want to think too much about what Thane's attention meant. She'd grown to love Montana and the ranch. If she were being honest, she'd also fallen in love with Thane. The depth of her emotions scared Sadie.

As long as Ezra stayed in San Francisco, returning wouldn't be possible for her. Even if he left, there was nothing for her in California. Her parents had tried to force her into marriage, and the few friends she'd made would side with Ezra. Given his wealth and plans to be governor, most would choose him over her.

What choices did she have with such a small amount of money? Sadie thought she might be able to obtain a job in Splendor. Maybe at the boardinghouse, the St. James, or one of the other shops. Doing laundry, cooking, or seamstress was well beyond her skills. She'd helped Selina with all three. Those experiences didn't mean she could do them on her own.

"The boys are going to clean up for lunch. Did you warm the stew?"

Selina pulled Sadie from her depressing thoughts of leaving the MacLaren ranch. "I'll go check on it. There's cornbread, too."

"Wonderful. Let's get the twins into the house, then I'll let the boys know their food is ready."

Sadie began to mentally catalogue everything she did. All the activities she'd miss after leaving the ranch. They seemed insignificant when studied one at a time. Together, they were memories to remember wherever she ended up.

"I don't want to leave." Sadie muttered the sentence over and over to herself until Selina returned with the men. "Beef stew and cornbread today."

Instead of grabbing a bowl, Thane waited until the others had taken their share. Stepping close, he made sure to brush his arm against hers as he scooped stew into his bowl.

Sitting together at the table, his thigh touched hers. "Let's take a walk when we're finished."

Bram arched a brow at him. "We've a lot to do before dark, lad."

"It'll be a short walk."

As Bram tried to object, he grimaced when Selina kicked his chin. "Fine. A short one."

Cleaning up took little time. Vince left the kitchen first, dashing down the outside steps to disappear into the barn.

Sadie watched him go, wishing they'd been able to find Kevin. "How's he doing, Bram?"

"Not good, lass. He's missing his brother."

"The main problem is he'll always wonder what happened to Kev. If he knew, the days might go better for him." Kissing Selina, Bram picked up his hat, following Vince outside.

"I wish there was something else we could do."

Thane took Sadie's hand. "Let's walk, lass."

"Are you all right with the twins, Selina?"

"Fine. And take a long walk. You both deserve it."

Thane led her to what he called the stables. It was on the other side of the house, hidden by large trees and broad bushes. She'd seen the structure before, never taking the time to ask about it.

"Why is it off by itself?"

"We use it for mares that will foal soon. Some people call them birthing barns. There are two stalls." He stopped outside a pair of wide doors.

"Have you ever had two mares in there at the same time?"

"Once. They foaled the same night. All four of us were in there for close to fifteen hours straight. This was after a full day working the ranch."

"Was Selina here?"

"Not then. It was several months later that she and Bram got married." He squeezed her hand. "Let's go inside."

Even midday, the structure was dark inside. Thane left the pair of doors open to let in the light.

"You can see everything from right here. In front of you are the stalls."

Her gaze wandered over the building's walls and roof. "They're bigger than I guessed."

"They have to be. There's the mare, plus two to three of us working with her. Finally, we're joined by the foal."

"It sounds exciting."

"It can be. Especially when the foal appears."

She walked several feet closer to one of the stalls, looking into the interior. "I'd love to be here to watch."

Coming up behind her, he rested his hands on her waist. "You can be here, Sadie."

Leaning back into him, her head rested against his shoulder. "I'll have to leave someday."

"Why? Is there someplace else you'd rather be?"

"Not really."

"You don't want to go back to San Francisco?" His hands moved to circle her waist from behind.

She shook her head. "No. There's nothing for me there."

"There's a lot for you here."

Turning in his arms, she studied his series features. "Such as?"

"Me, for one. We haven't known each other long enough to commit, but I want more time with you. I believe we could have a future together, Sadie."

"There's so much I don't know about you."

"A good reason to stay. We'd have time to get to know each other. And there's Selina. She could use your help and your friendship. There are times we ride out and don't come back for a few days. Besides taking care of the twins, there are animals to feed, eggs to gather, cooking, laundry, and cleaning. It would be a lot for one woman."

Arms around his waist, she met his gaze. "So you want me to stay to help Selina?" Her grin softened the question.

"I want you here because I can't imagine this ranch without you."

"You know there's a chance I'll leave anyway. Maybe I won't like living on a ranch. You might discover a city girl isn't who you want. Anything could happen."

"We may also find we're good for each other. You might fall in love with me."

Laughing, she shoved his chest. "Has anyone ever called you arrogant?"

"I suppose so. Just not to my face."

He laughed with her. In Thane's mind, she was already the perfect woman for him. He just needed time to prove he was the perfect man for her.

Chapter Nineteen

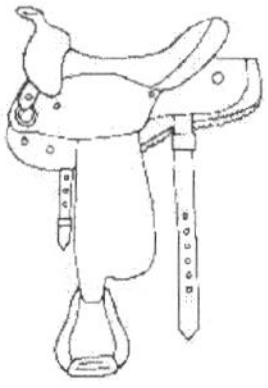

Martha read the latest letter from the couple in Big Pine, her hope of finding a manager for the home for orphans plummeting. She'd agreed to manage the Splendor home until a manager was hired. It appeared her work might be a long way from ending.

The orphans from Big Pine were to arrive within a few hours. The beds were made, food stored in the kitchen, and the schoolroom furnished with more desks and chairs.

The town leaders had agreed to continue the school in Splendor, allowing Martha to bring the orphans to town each day. Rose Keenan would continue as the teacher, while Amelia would become the cook at the orphan home. They'd share the housekeeping duties.

"Martha?" Amelia stood in the doorway to the room which had become the office.

"Do you need help?"

"No. Everything for supper is ready. I'll heat it up once the children arrive. Deputy Morgan Wheeler?"

"Of course. Why?"

"The sheriff asked him to ride out and make sure everything was ready for the children. He's in the living room."

"Wonderful." Martha followed Amelia down the hall to see the deputy looking out of a large window in the living room. "Hello, Deputy Wheeler."

Whirling around, he smiled. "Miss van Plew. I hope I'm not interrupting your work."

"Not at all. Would you like a tour?"

"If you have time."

"I have a few items needing attention, but Amelia has a few minutes." She hadn't missed the way her new cook flushed when mentioning Morgan. Nor how the deputy sent secret looks at Amelia.

"I'd be happy to give the deputy a tour. We'll start upstairs." She motioned for him to follow her up the staircase. Reaching the landing, she made a turn toward the front of the house. "This is one of the bedrooms. We have three stacked beds, with one below and one above. It gives us six beds in this room. Noah Brandt came up with the idea. What do you think?"

He quickly tore his gaze from her to focus on the beds. "Smart idea. I understand Noah has a lot of them. I live in one of his houses with Tucker and Jonas."

"Yes, I know."

"You do?"

"I mean, there isn't much privacy in Splendor. Everyone seems to know what the rest of us are doing." She touched her cheek, feeling the warmth. "There I go, rambling on. I'll show you the rest of the rooms upstairs." She passed in front of him, not seeing his smile.

"How many children do you expect will live here?"

"Ruth Paige and Martha planned for up to twenty-four. Twelve boys and twelve girls. Six children in each bedroom. I'm not sure how that will work. I'd think it would be better to have all the girls in one room. Same with the boys."

"It wouldn't be hard to change the upstairs. Remove walls to combine bedrooms. Might make it easier to check on them."

"Rose and I were thinking the same. We planned to talk to Ruth and Martha as the number of children increases. I'll show you the remaining rooms downstairs."

"Last fall, I rode by here on the way to another ranch. It wasn't in good shape. You've done a good job fixing it up."

"All of this was Martha and Ruth's doing. With a lot of work from Noah and a few men he hired. This is the library and game room."

Morgan's eyes widened the instant he stepped into the room. "This is a real library." Making a turn around the room, he stopped to pull out a book. "This may be bigger than the library in town."

"Do you enjoy reading?"

Morgan nodded, sliding out another book. "I've always read. My mother would have to make threats to get me outside." He chuckled. "I'd sneak out a book, find a tree, and read for as long as I could. What about you, Amelia? Are you a reader?"

"I am. From what Ruth has said, she and Reverend Paige have collected books since they were first married. No matter where they were sent, the books went with them. Most of these came from her home. There are even books from the seventeen hundreds. Most are about the war for independence from England. I'm sure they'd let you borrow any book in the library. Are you ready to see the rest?"

"I'll follow you."

Walking to the back, she stopped. "This is all mine."

"This is a huge kitchen. Will you do all the cooking?"

"Except the one day I don't work."

"Which is?"

"Sunday. I sing in the choir." Amelia shrugged.

"I've seen you. Can't say as I've heard you, as everyone blends together. Are you cooking for the children today?"

"Fruit bread when they arrive, and supper after they put their belongings away."

"Will you live here?"

"Yes. There's a bedroom behind the kitchen. It's bigger than the one I shared with Rose at the St. James."

"Are you happy with your decision to leave the Eagle's Nest?"

Amelia looked around the kitchen, a smile growing as her gaze landed on the new stove. "The children haven't arrived yet, but so far, it has been a good decision."

Leaving the kitchen, she walked toward the living room, pointing out Martha's office, and a large supply room. Stopping in the parlor, she looked out the window in time to see a covered wagon stop outside.

"They're here," Amelia breathed out. "I'll get Martha."

"I'll help the children." Morgan watched her for a moment before heading outside.

Morgan and Amelia sat at the small table in the kitchen, eating their roasted chicken, potatoes, and vegetable casserole. Martha had given her the recipe, and the vegetables from her root cellar.

"This is real good," Morgan said between bites. "Did you learn to cook from your mother?"

Amelia's expression didn't change. "Until I was ten. That's when she passed away."

Setting down his fork, he looked at her. "I'm real sorry, Amelia."

"Thank you. It was a long time ago."

"It must've been hard. Were you an only child?"

She nodded. "I didn't think Papa would ever get over her death. He didn't turn to drink." Pursing her lips, she stared at her plate. "He was just...gone." She touched a finger to her temple. "Eventually, he met a woman and married her. I was sixteen."

"Did you get along with her?"

"I thought we did. When she moved in, she took over the cooking. Wouldn't even let me help. Then she talked Papa into sending me to a boarding school for girls in the next town over. I stayed a few months before running away. It took him months to find me at his sister's house in New York. She helped me finish school and complete enough additional education to be a teacher. My aunt was good friends with Rachel Pelletier's family. That was how we met."

"And what eventually got you to Splendor." Morgan grinned at her.

"You've heard the story."

"Heard it within a week of arriving in town. It's a good story. Do you still write your father?"

"I tried for a while, but he never wrote back. My guess is his wife threw my letters away. At least once a month, I send a letter to my aunt. I'm trying to talk her and her husband into visiting. They never had children, so I became their surrogate daughter."

"Amelia, the children are ready for dessert." Martha picked up one of the pies. "They loved supper."

"The vegetable casserole recipe you gave me was excellent." Amelia lifted the second pie. "Morgan, would you mind bringing out those small plates?"

He picked them up with one hand, grabbing the serving knife next to them. It took no more than ten minutes for Morgan to serve everyone, including the wagon driver, a large slice of pie.

Pulling up a chair, he looked at the children. Morgan knew they'd been expecting six orphans. When the wagon stopped, seven children climbed down.

The ride from Big Pine in the large Conestoga wagon had been an adventure, one they'd talk about for a while. The owner, who'd also been the driver, explained the couple who managed the Big Pine home wanted to send one wagon large enough for each child's belongings.

Morgan wondered about each of their stories. What had brought them to the home? Had their parents died, or were they part of the growing number of children who weren't wanted? He thought of the circumstances that would push a parent into giving up their son or daughter. Morgan couldn't imagine giving up his own child.

"I want more," one of the children said around his last bite.

"Sorry, partner," Morgan answered. "There isn't any left."

The boy didn't complain, just pushed his plate a few inches away. He guessed him to be six or seven, with sandy blond hair and freckles across his nose.

Martha shoved her chair away from the table and stood. "All right, everyone. It's time to clean up and get ready for bed."

Without a word of protest, they picked up their plates and forks, returning them to the kitchen before heading upstairs. Martha, Amelia, and Morgan watched them walk off, resigned yet determined expressions on each face.

"They're not what I expected. But I don't know much about children."

"This is their first day, Morgan. We'll see how they act after they've been here a while. I believe I'll go upstairs to check on them, Amelia. Do you mind cleaning up the kitchen?"

"Not at all. Are you staying the night, Martha?"

"Yes. I want to help get them organized in the morning. Rose will be here early. I'm a little surprised she didn't come out today."

"She still needed to pack. I'm certain she'll be here early tomorrow to prepare the lessons for today. If she doesn't make it in time, I'll do my best to help out."

"You're a Godsend, Amelia."

Morgan's gaze moved from Martha to Amelia. "I'll help you with cleaning up before riding back to town." He followed her into the kitchen.

"Nonsense. Cleaning isn't your job."

"I don't mind." Morgan didn't explain being with her was much better than spending the evening with his two roommates. "I'll wash. You can dry and put them away."

Amelia studied him a moment, deciding whether or not to say something about his bossiness. Letting out a slow breath, she grabbed a towel and a large plate. This would be her opportunity to learn more about the deputy.

"Did you help at home?"

"Growing up, you mean? Yes. Everyone had day chores and evening chores. Pa was ill much of the time, so we took over most of his work."

She placed a dried dish on a shelf. "Did you have a large family?"

"Two brothers and two sisters. I'm the middle brother. The girls are younger than me and my brothers."

"What about your mother?"

"She died when the youngest girl was born." Glancing around the kitchen, he dried his hands. "That's all of them. I'd best get back to town."

Rushing to follow him out of the kitchen, she almost rammed into his back when he stopped to pick up his hat. Settling it on his head, he turned to looked at her.

"Thank you for supper. You're a real good cook, Amelia."

"You're welcome. I hope you'll give Sheriff Evans a good report on our progress."

"It will be an excellent report." He continued to stand there, watching her before clearing his throat. Opening his mouth, he shut it, shaking his head. "Good evening, Amelia."

"Good evening, Morgan."

She stood on the porch, watching him ride off until he disappeared around a bend in the trail. "Interesting man," Amelia muttered before entering the house, her mind already on the children.

Chapter Twenty

Eyes closed, Sadie stretched both arms above her head, the knuckles of both hands touching the headboard. She thought of the day before, a smile touching the corners of her mouth.

Thane had taken her to lunch at the boardinghouse restaurant and to the St. James for an early supper. Both places were wonderful in their own unique ways. Being with Thane had made the entire day special.

Sadie lingered in bed a few more minutes before pulling back the covers. Taking more time than usual for morning ablutions and to dress, her mind settled on Thane.

She liked him. No, more than liked. Not love, though. It was too soon to have such deep feelings for the handsome rancher. Maybe what lodged in her chest was...

"Gratitude?" Shaking her head, she dismissed the idea.

A soft knock on the door dashed the path her mind had taken. Rushing to the door, she opened it to see Thane. Before she knew his intentions, he kissed her cheek.

"Good morning, Miss Thompson." The smile he gave her caused a tingling sensation in her stomach.

"Good morning, Mr. MacLaren." As she spoke, Sadie noticed how dark it was outside. "Is it morning?"

"Almost. We're riding out to bring in some stray cattle. Selina isn't awake, but the twins are a little restless."

"I'll take care of them." Closing the door behind her, she stepped past him toward Selina and Bram's bedroom. Taking a quick look, she relaxed. Both were cooing while playing with their feet.

"We'll be fine until Selina wakes up."

"I'm awake, Sadie." The covers moved, but Selina didn't sit up. "I decided to stay in bed until they start fussing."

"Good idea. I'll take care of their diapers while you get ready to feed them."

"Thanks, Sadie." Selina pulled the covers back over her head.

Closing the bedroom door, Sadie smiled at a grinning Thane. "We're fine. Go ahead and do what you need to."

When he bent toward her this time, he brushed a kiss across her lips before wrapping her in his arms. The next kiss, warm and deep, had her toes curling. When it ended, her entire body, head to the soles of her feet, tingled.

"I have to leave." He breathed out the sentence as he stepped away. "We'll be back before sunset."

Nodding, she didn't move as he rushed down the stairs.

San Francisco

Ezra Crockett's pen hovered over the piece of paper, struggling to write a reply to Agent Beardsley. The man would expect a courteous, professional response. Ezra didn't have one for him. His thoughts were filled with the rage he felt at learning Sophrona's protector was none other than the sheriff of Splendor. The man required verified proof of the theft, including evidence Sophrona was the thief.

There'd been a day not too long ago, when he could've talked one or two of his staff to testify against Sophrona. Cutting pay for everyone, and firing laggards, turned those left against him. Plus, they all loved Sophrona.

"Everyone loved her," he sneered, staring at the blank sheet of paper.

Setting down the pen, Ezra leaned back in his chair, focusing on the painting of a scantily dressed woman. He'd purchased the oversized piece of art from a saloon owner who needed cash. The man had all but cried when Ezra's hired help loaded it into the carriage.

The woman in the painting continued to intrigue him. According to the previous owner, she had worked at another saloon in San Francisco for a year before disappearing. He didn't know of a single person who'd seen her since.

Because of the scant amount of history, Ezra had a habit of making up tales involving the woman. He'd let his imagination flow in any and all directions. The odd habit always relaxed him.

Blinking several times, he broke the spell to stare down at the blank paper. Picking up the pen, he wrote. It took less than a minute to complete the telegram to Beardsley.

The answer to his dilemma had been in his head all along. If the job proved too difficult for his hired men, he'd move to the obvious solution. Ezra would bring Sophrona back to San Francisco himself.

St. Louis

Cole watched Dante as the curious boy moved from one aisle to the next, looking for anything left behind by a previous traveler. Other passengers watched, also, most amused at his actions. So far, Dante had found two playing cards, one cuff link, a woman's calling card, and a pair of dice. A pretty good haul for the eight-year-old.

Dante wasn't his son by birth. The paper in Cole's pocket affirmed the young boy was now his responsibility. A heartfelt vow to a woman he'd once loved came to fruition, and blood or not, Cole felt a tug in his chest each time he looked at Dante. A son not by birth, but by circumstances.

"Papa, look at this."

Glancing at Dante's open palm, he straightened in his seat. "Do you know what it is?"

"No, Papa."

"That is a .44 caliber bullet. How about I keep it safe for you?"

"With everything else?"

Cole's features softened. "Yes. I'll keep it with the rest of your loot in my satchel."

Brows drawn together, Dante studied the bullet for a moment before giving it to Cole. "What is loot?"

Shoving the bullet into a pocket, he thought of how to answer. "Loot is what is taken during conflicts between two opposing groups. Do you know anything about the war between the states?"

Dante returned a vigorous nod. "Mama told me about it. Unions and Confederates." A light seemed to flash in the boy's eyes. "The Unions took loot from the Confederates?"

"Or the Confederates took loot from the Union soldiers. It's just an example."

Dante seemed to consider this for a bit before whirling around to continue his search.

"He sure is a well-behaved boy."

Cole turned to see a short, stout man with a trimmed white beard and mustache standing in the aisle. "Yes, he is. He's also very active."

"Ah, yes. Young boys can run you in circles." There was a wistful tone in the man's voice, making Cole wonder if he had sons of his own. "What's his name?"

"Dante. He's eight."

"Well, you take good care of Dante." The man turned, walking back to his seat.

"Yes, sir. I will."

The conductor entered their car, watched Dante for a moment before announcing St. Louis was up ahead. Cole planned to eat in the bustling city and let Dante expel some of his stored up energy before reboarding the train.

St. Louis hadn't changed much since Cole had been there a few years earlier. There were more buildings and a lot more people. There'd been a time when he thought a city similar to St. Louis would be the right place to settle down. After a few weeks in Splendor, he'd changed his mind. He hoped Dante would adjust with little effort.

"Where are we going, Papa?"

His chest squeezed once more, the same as it did each time Dante called him his father. "We're going to have lunch at a restaurant up ahead." He nodded to the large hotel a block away.

"Mama used to take me to lunch. We always had to have Grandpa or Grandma with us."

Dante didn't have to finish for Cole to know what he meant. Evelyn had left home to get away from their overbearing ways. She feared returning would mean an end to her freedom. It appeared her fears were justified.

"From now on, it's you and me, Dante."

The boy flashed a smile, which ripped a hole in his chest. "Can I order what I want?"

"Let's see what they're offering."

Dante slipped his hand into Cole's. "All right."

Martha finished entering the last amounts in the journal before sliding it back into the desk drawer. She was amazed how much food the children could eat. In three days, they'd eaten what Amelia had planned for five days. Martha had arrived this morning with a wagon laden with food, clothing, and the materials required for a set of four swings.

Part of the order had a great deal to do with the telegram Ruth had received the day before. The Big Pine home was sending over three more children via the regular stagecoach between the two towns. The couple managing the home didn't provide ages, but did indicate they were siblings. They were still well under what the Splendor home could accept.

Rising from her chair, she walked to the window. The children were playing a modified version of baseball with a pitcher, first, second, and third basemen, plus batters. They rotated through positions with so much ease, Martha guessed they learned the game at the home in Big Pine.

The daily routine had come together as she and Ruth had planned. The three additional children arriving in a few hours shouldn't cause any issues. Being siblings would help.

Turning away from the window, Martha left the office, locking the door behind her. She and Ruth had keys, as did Noah Brandt, since he and his wife, Abigail, had purchased the house for use as a home for orphans.

She didn't stop at the kitchen, walking through the living room, and exiting through the front door. The wraparound porch was magnificent. Noah had provided a dozen chairs and a few tables. The perfect place to relax.

Selecting one of the rocking chairs, she sat down, closing her eyes. Martha allowed her thoughts to drift to Cole. His quick departure from Splendor still bothered her.

She'd refrained from asking Gabe or his deputies where Cole had gone. If he'd wanted her to know, he would've told her. There'd been no telegrams or letters. Nothing at all from the man she'd allowed herself to love.

A cold niggling sensation started in her spine, spreading upward to the base of her skull. It was familiar. Since childhood, whenever she experienced the icy flash of warning, bad news had followed. This time, Martha believed she understood what it meant.

Cole wouldn't be returning.

Chapter Twenty-One

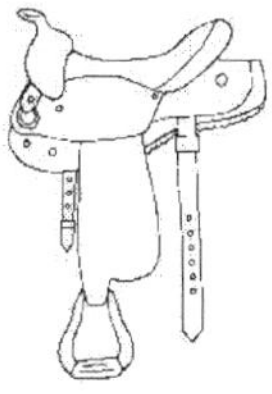

MacLaren Ranch

"That's it, Sadie. Relax and don't forget to breathe." Thane jogged outside the corral fence, keeping pace with her horse. "Keep your heels down. If you squeeze his sides with your legs, he'll go faster."

"I don't want faster," she shouted back at him. "Walking is fine."

"For now. You'll be ready to trot by tomorrow." He continued to keep pace with her as she completed a seventh round inside the corral. The gelding had moved from a slow to a fast walk. A trivial difference from a trot.

Not answering, Sadie concentrated on the position of her hands, legs, and her posture. When the gelding moved into a trot, all she could do was hold on.

"Thane!"

"You're doing fine, Sadie. If you want to stop, relax your legs, pull back on the reins, and say *whoa*."

"Whoa! Whoa! Whoa!"

He'd tell her later that all she needed was one command. For now, he wanted her to enjoy what she'd accomplished.

Slipping through the slats of the fence, he took the reins, helping her dismount. "You did real well, Sadie. You're a natural rider."

"I don't know about that, but it was fun." Face flushed, her broad smile landed on him. "Thank you, Thane."

"Anytime you want to ride, just let me know. If I'm not here, anyone else will saddle a horse for you."

"I'll wait until you're around."

He liked the sound of that. "Fine with me. Come on. You can help with the tack and grooming him."

Sadie stroked a hand along the horse's back. "What's his name?"

"Cotton."

"Cotton?"

"He was white as cotton at birth. At least that's what Selina told us. We bought him from her family at Redemption's Edge. We didn't bring a remuda with us when we rode out from California."

"A remuda?"

"A string of saddle-broke horses. Ranch hands choose which one to ride each day. They're also used on a long ride to give the regular mount a break. We bought four horses from the Pelletiers not long after we arrived. Cotton is about nine years old and well broke. He'd be a good horse for you, Sadie."

"If I stay."

"Yes. If you stay."

Neither said more about the future as they removed the saddle and remaining tack, groomed Cotton, and let him loose in the pasture behind the barn. Stepping onto the lowest rung of the fence, Sadie rested her arms on the top rail.

"Did you pick out Cotton?"

"With Bram. We had to agree on the four horses." He joined her on the fence. "The Pelletiers breed fine horses. We're partners with them in filling orders for the government."

"Selina mentioned the contracts. She said there was more work than both ranches could handle."

"Not yet, but we're getting close. The problem is rounding up more horses. We've been filling the contracts with bands of wild horses. The herd moves every day. They're ruled by a stallion, and he'll do whatever he can to avoid capture."

"Do you ever return without wild horses?"

"Too often. We'll stay out as long as a week. If we return empty-handed, we'll work the ranch for a day or two, then ride out again."

Sadie remained silent for a couple minutes as she watched Cotton. "Is it just the two of you who search for horses?"

"Travis Dixon and Wyatt Jackson usually ride with us. Both work for the Pelletiers. Bram and I will be heading out in a few days. We could be gone a week or more."

"Selina told me it would be soon. Bram shouldn't worry. Between the two of us, Connor and Audrey will be fine."

"I believe he'll miss the babes more than worry about them."

Stepping to the ground, Sadie took another look at Cotton. "I need to help Selina with the twins and get lunch ready. Thanks again for the lesson."

"Anytime." He watched until she disappeared into the kitchen.

Cheyenne

"Do we get to ride in one of those, Papa?" Dante pointed toward the stagecoach down the street.

"We sure do. It's a stagecoach. If they have room for us, we'll be taking it all the way to Splendor. Should we find out if there are seats?"

Dante nodded vigorously before taking off at a run.

Cole hurried to catch him before his son collided with a horse or wagon. Wrapping an arm around him, he swung Dante into the air before setting him on his feet.

"Remember what I told you in St. Louis about not rushing into the streets?"

Dante stared at the new boots Cole had bought him. "Watch for riders and wagons."

"Did you watch this time?"

He shook his head. "No."

"All right. Let's try again with you looking for anything which could run you over."

Watching for riders and those driving wagons, Dante waited for a big opening before dashing across the rutted, dirt street. Stopping on the boardwalk, he raised his hands in the air in triumph.

Cole couldn't describe what the boy's exuberant smile did to him. He wondered if real fathers experienced such intense feelings for their children. He supposed most did.

Joining Dante in front of the stagecoach office, he paid for two tickets to Splendor.

"It'll be a full coach," the clerk said as he held out a piece of paper. "Give that to the driver. Is that all your luggage?" He nodded toward the two satchels Cole held in each hand.

"Yes."

"Give them to the driver. He'll put them up top. The stage leaves in thirty minutes. He won't wait if you aren't here."

"Thanks. We'll wait in front."

"Suit yourself." The clerk moved down the counter to help another customer.

"Okay if I leave these in the corner?"

The clerk waved a hand indicating to put them behind the counter, never stopping his conversation with the other customer.

Outside, Cole looked around. He'd been through Cheyenne before, had talked to the sheriff about a deputy position. Deciding to continue on to Splendor, he turned down the offer.

Spotting the general store across the street, he placed a hand on Dante's shoulder. "Let's see what's over there." Stepping into the street, he came to an abrupt halt at the sight of three riders entering Cheyenne.

Faces shadowed by hats, Cole didn't recognize any of them until his gaze landed on ivory handled matching six-shooters worn by the rider in the middle.

"I'll be." Squeezing Dante's shoulder. "There's someone I want you to meet."

Dante's eyes tracked the three riders as they came closer. When they reined up a few feet away, he shifted closer to Cole.

"If it isn't Columbus Santori. I thought my eyesight was going." The man slung his right leg over his horse's neck, sliding to the ground. "How are you, Cole?"

"Good, Moses. I didn't recognize you until I saw your guns."

Moses's hands touched the ivory handles. "Best friends I ever had. Who's your partner?"

"This is my son, Dante. Dante, this is Moses Stone."

Dante stepped forward, holding out his hand. "Pleased to meet you, Mr. Stone."

The stunned expression on Moses's face faded as he shook Dante's small hand. "Good to meet you, son." He motioned toward the others, who'd joined them on the boardwalk. "These are my cousins. Solomon Vance and Eli Green. Boys, this is Cole Santori and his son, Dante."

Introductions made, Cole and Moses had little time to catch up before the stage driver walked from behind the office.

"You men taking the stage?"

"Just me and my son. I'll get our satchels."

"The ones behind the counter?"

Cole nodded.

"I already put them up top. We'll be leaving in ten minutes. It's a full coach, so you should claim your seats early."

"Thanks." Cole turned back to Moses. "Lousy timing."

"Where are you headed?" Moses asked.

"Splendor, Montana. About half a day's ride west of Big Pine."

"We may be heading your way after a few days here. The three of us just left the Rangers, and aren't too keen on riding east."

"You'd better ask for me if you get to Splendor. Are you looking for work?"

"Not yet. I heard you're a deputy."

"Sure am. Sheriff's a good man."

Moses glanced at the others, lowering his voice. "We're hunting two men who killed friends of ours. We won't be lighting anywhere for long until we find the men." He slid wanted posters from a pocket. "Keep a look out for these two. They're real nasty."

"I will. Thanks."

"Those taking the stage need to board now!" The driver's voice boomed with authority.

“Wish we had time for a beer, Moses. It’s darn good to see you.”

“Same here. Have a safe trip.” He nodded toward Dante. “Nice to meet you, young man.”

“Yes, sir.”

“Watch your backs, Cole. I meant it when I said the men we’re tracking are dangerous. They don’t care how or who they go after as long as the money is good.”

Moses’s warning stuck with Cole all the way to Big Pine, where he took time to locate Sheriff Parker Sterling. After introducing Dante, he shared the information from Moses.

“My friend had wanted posters.”

“I’ll check the pile. Sure don’t need any more trouble in Big Pine. I’m getting too old for this job.”

Saying their goodbyes, Dante boarded the stagecoach ahead of Cole. He slid to the opposite side, peering out the opening. Four more people climbed aboard, three sitting across from them, while the fourth sat next to Cole. The driver closed the door before climbing up to his seat. Beside him, another man held a shotgun.

A few seconds passed before the team of horses headed north out of Cheyenne. Cole knew they were about to enter territory populated by Crow, Sioux, and Shoshone. The trail between Cheyenne and Big Pine was unpredictable and dangerous.

There were times the tribes allowed the stage to pass without incident. It meant nothing. A few days later, the stage would be attacked. Drivers, guards, and passengers knew to stay on alert.

“Papa, look.” Dante pointed to a hill a mile away. A dozen warriors sat on their horses.

“Change places with me, son.” The moment he settled by the window, Cole pulled his gun from its holster.

An instant later, the warriors flew down the hill, their war cries loud enough to be heard inside the stage.

Chapter Twenty-Two

MacLaren Ranch

"Do you mind hanging out the laundry while I feed the twins?" Selina held Connor against her breast while Audrey lay in a crate lined with blankets.

"Not at all." Picking up a large basket, Sadie headed outside. "I shouldn't be long."

She stepped into a glorious spring day. Inhaling, Sadie took a moment to admire the vast expanse of land, the snow-capped mountains to the west.

Hanging the laundry, she thought of the differences in her two worlds. San Francisco and Splendor were complete opposites in every way.

One, a thriving city on the ocean with wealth, poverty, crowding, and stately homes. The other, a growing frontier town with plenty of room, industrious people, and a heart to help those in need.

Sadie had heard about the home for orphans started by a few local women. Selina had shared other stories of how the town had come together to face hardship. She wondered if those living in San Francisco would come together so eagerly.

Ezra Crockett solved problems by dispensing money, never bothering to get his hands dirty helping those in need. Those activities were left to others.

The men and women she'd met in Splendor might not have much money to contribute. What they did possess were their skills and time. In her mind, those were more important than all the money in Ezra's bank.

Leaving the laundry basket on the ground, she meant to watch Cotton for a few minutes when the sound of pounding hooves on the hard ground caught her attention. Shading her eyes with a hand, she squinted. The bright, early morning sun was at her back, but it didn't help her identify the rider.

Closing the distance between them, the man lifted a hand to wave, then reined up at the sight of Selina holding a rifle. Stopping about twenty feet from the kitchen's back door, he removed his hat.

"You must be Selina, Bram's wife. I'm Sean MacLaren, Bram and Thane's cousin."

Lowering the rifle, she leaned it against the railing before dashing down the steps. "Sean MacLaren. We expected you weeks ago. Rather, we expected your friend who traveled back with you."

Dismounting, he gave her a robust hug. "Aye. There was a change in plans. I'll explain everything." Walking over to Sadie, he looked her up and down. "And you must be Sadie. Thane sent me a letter, telling me about your struggles. I'm Sean."

"It's good to meet you, Sean. Did you ride out alone from California?"

"I did. May I put up my horse in your barn?"

Sadie looked at Selina, who nodded. "Of course. The stall at the far end isn't being used."

"When you're done, come into the house. Lunch isn't ready yet, but we have coffee and sweet bread."

"Thank you. I'm starving."

As he walked into the barn, Sadie moved closer to Selina. "He does have a resemblance to both Bram and Thane."

"According to Bram, Sean is one of their favorite cousins. He returned a few months ago from several years attending veterinary school in Scotland. A friend of his returned with him. That's who I thought would be moving to Splendor."

"Do you mean Sean is here to stay?"

"That's what Bram told me. The town doesn't have a veterinarian, so Sean will be educating the townsfolk, as well as treating animals. This is very exciting."

"He is quite handsome, isn't he?"

"I won't tell Thane you asked, but yes, he is a good-looking man. As are all the MacLaren men I've met." Hearing the twins fuss, she picked up the shotgun. "I'd better get inside with the twins."

Returning to the clothesline, Sadie picked up the laundry basket, then set it back down. She still had to feed the chickens and collect any new eggs. Lifting her skirt, she did her best to avoid the soggy ground from the rain a week earlier.

Opening the door to the chicken coop, she looked around, froze, then screamed.

A man, wearing not a lick of clothes and dirtier than anyone Sadie had ever seen, curled into himself in a corner of the coop. Her scream startled him. Shifting until his chest faced the corner, he wrapped his arms around his shivering body.

Grabbing a couple of saddle blankets, she inched forward, focusing on the man's face. Emaciated and sunburned to a deep red, he refused to look at her. Still, there was something about him.

Getting to within a few feet of him, Sadie bent down, draping one blanket over his shoulders. The second went over his legs. He grabbed the edges, pulling them around his body.

Though she was far from certain, Sadie lowered her voice, taking a chance. "Kevin?"

His body jerked.

"Kevin, is that you?"

Opening his mouth, an ear-piercing keening noise burst out. The short distance between them allowed Sadie to study his cracked and swollen lips, the bruising around his eyes, and scrapes down his chest and arms.

"Kevin, I'm Sadie. Do you remember me?"

His eyes met hers for a moment before he shook his head vigorously.

The denial didn't change the fact the man on the dirt floor was Kevin.

"I'm going to get you some clothes. Stay here until I get back. I won't be gone long."

Standing, she whirled around, holding back a shriek when she spotted Sean in the shed's doorway. Pressing a hand to her chest, she stopped a foot away.

Sean peered around her. "Who is that man?"

"I'm almost certain he's our missing ranch hand, Kevin Latham. His brother, Vince, and a lot of others have been searching for him. Do you mind watching him? I'm going to get some of his clothes. Perhaps we can get him to go inside."

"How long has he been missing?"

"At least a month. He and Vince were searching for strays, got separated, and Kevin disappeared. It happened during a storm. Thane said any tracks had washed away." She shot a look at Kevin. "I'd better get the clothes."

When she closed the door, he took a couple steps closer to Kevin. Letting his gaze wander over the much too skinny ranch hand, he found himself wondering where he'd been the last month.

Reaching out, Sean touched one of the long gashes on his arm. "How did you get these?"

Kevin lifted one shoulder in a shrug.

"Appears you may have taken a fall. Is that what happened?"

Kevin pressed his lips together before giving a slow nod.

"Did you fall more than once?"

He nodded again.

"When was the last time you ate?"

The shrug came slower. This time, when he raised his face, Kevin's eyes were glassy and distant.

"Do you remember when you last ate?"

Kevin gave another slow shake of his head.

Seconds later, the door flew open. Selina stood part inside and part out, staring at the gaunt figure of a man. "It *is* Kevin." Juggling Connor on her hip while holding pants and a shirt, she slowly approached him. "How is he, Sean?"

"I've gotten a couple answers. The scrapes on his arms and chest are from falls. He doesn't know when he last ate."

"Sadie is making him eggs. Do you think he could drink milk or coffee?"

"Let's try milk first."

"Milk."

Sean and Selina shot surprised looks at Kevin.

"That's right. Milk." Sean watched Kevin's eyes flash for the briefest second before he stared down at the ground. "Let's get him dressed and into the house. After he eats, I'll get him cleaned up. It wouldn't surprise me if he sleeps for hours."

"I wish Vince were here." Selina tucked the bed cover under Kevin's chin.

Sadie nodded. "Maybe the men will get back early."

"Thank you for cleaning him up, Sean." Selina's features were serene as she watched Kevin breathe.

"Glad I was here to help. He's been through quite a bit. What he needs now is rest."

Selina touched Kevin's forehead. "It's a miracle he isn't hot. He's lost so much weight."

"It won't take him long to gain it back. You should stay with soup for now. I'm going to put away my horse and bring in the saddlebags. Is there a bedroom I can use? If not, I can bunk down in the barn."

Selina motioned for him to follow her. "There's a bedroom. I'll show you." She'd made up the bed while Sean bathed and dressed Kevin.

"We should take him to the doctor tomorrow. There is a doctor in Splendor, right?"

Opening the bedroom door, she laughed. "We have a real nice clinic with two excellent doctors. You and Sadie can take the wagon into town right after breakfast."

"Will you be all right here with the twins?"

"I wouldn't have told you to go if I wasn't. Sadie can introduce you to the sheriff and a few others while you're there." Hearing the babies fuss, she stepped into the hall. "You are staying, aren't you?"

Sean flashed her a bright smile. "I'm planning to start Splendor's first veterinary clinic. Hope the town's ready for it."

Chapter Twenty-Three

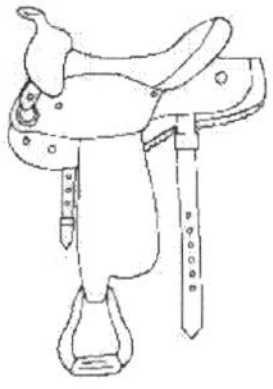

Vince swung his rope into the air, driving the horses into a canyon. Thane did the same on the other side of the herd while Bram drove them from the back. The horses and stallion gathered at the end of the one way canyon, allowing the men to get a count on what they'd achieved.

Thane added up the number of animals. "I count twenty head, Bram."

"Aye. That's my count, too. Travis?"

"Twenty head by my count. How do you want to do this?"

Checking the sun's location in the sky, Bram calculated the hours required to drive the horses to the MacLaren ranch versus Redemption's Edge.

"My guess is four hours to your place," Wyatt Jackson said. "Longer to the Pelletier ranch. Plus, there's a steep gorge we'll have to drive them around on the way to Redemption's Edge."

Bram knew whichever ranch they chose, the odds were the stallion would escape, then plague them with attempts to free his herd. Avoiding natural barriers, such as the gorge Wyatt mentioned, would help keep the horses together.

"We'll keep them in the canyon overnight and leave at first light." Bram watched the stallion dance in front of the herd. "Let's put up the barrier."

Travis and Wyatt had devised a system of ropes strung back and forth across the entrance to any area holding horses. The ropes weren't strong enough to contain a charging horse, but served as a visual barrier that worked a decent percentage of the time.

They rotated guarding the herd, three on while two ate and rested around a campfire. By morning, the men were ready to move the horses to the MacLaren ranch.

They used ropes to contain the stallion on the drive. The method required two men to ride alongside the horse while the other three stayed with the herd. It wasn't foolproof, and more than one man had been injured when the stallion reared back, tearing away from its bindings.

Several hours into the drive, the group spotted the afternoon stage heading into Splendor from Salt Lake City. Holding up, the men circled the horses while Travis and Wyatt tossed two more loops of rope around the stallion.

Watching from a distance, they raised their hands to the driver. Inside the coach, Thane counted four people. Two men faced a young couple on the opposite bench seat. He wondered if the four were passing through or planned to make Splendor their home.

Waiting until the stagecoach was out of sight, the men got the herd moving once again. If all went well, they'd be at the MacLaren ranch well before nightfall.

Ezra Crockett watched the group of men and horses until the stagecoach moved out of sight. Their appearance created a nice break from what had become a monotonous trip between Salt Lake City and Splendor. So far, he'd seen nothing to help him understand why anyone would want to create a life so far from civilization.

How could a woman as refined as Sophrona even consider giving up San Francisco for the hostile world of western Montana? Ezra thought of the week to come. He'd given himself seven days to locate Sophrona and get them both on a stage for California.

Adjusting himself to ease the growing pain in his back, his eyes widened. Pacing the stage was a group of five Indians. Heart racing, he pounded on the side of the stagecoach, getting the driver's attention. When the stage didn't slow, he yelled.

"What are those?"

Several moments passed before the driver bent down to yell back. "Look like Crow to me."

"What should we do?"

"Nothing."

"Nothing?" Ezra couldn't imagine doing nothing with several Crow following them. By the looks on the faces of the other three passengers, they were as confused as him.

"They ain't bothering us." The driver waited a few minutes before adding, "We're almost in Splendor."

The Crow rode off as if they'd heard the driver's words. Ezra relaxed, as did the other passengers.

The church's steeple came into view first. Resisting the urge to stick his head out the window, Ezra kept his excitement to himself. It wasn't the town that gave him a jolt. The fact he was closer to finding Sophrona is what heated his blood.

She'd eluded him for too long. It still baffled him how one small, young woman could outwit two hired guns. This had been followed by the sheriff refusing to hand her over to the Pinkerton agent, citing a lack of evidence. Weren't small town lawmen supposed to enforce wanted posters without asking questions? The fact he'd been outsmarted by a backwoods sheriff located in a podunk town still angered him.

It would be different now. Ezra would succeed where his hired guns had not.

When the stage stopped, he exited, glancing around to decide where to go first. Spotting the St. James hotel, he picked up his two satchels. Marching along the boardwalk, he noted the various businesses, his gaze stopping on the jail.

"No better time than now," he muttered, picking up his pace.

He was gratified to find the sheriff sitting at his desk. Dropping the satchels onto a nearby chair, he held out his hand.

"Name's Ezra Crockett, Sheriff."

The man behind the desk set down the paper he'd been reading. He stood, towering over the more diminutive Ezra and grasped the outstretched hand.

"Deputy Cash Coulter, Mr. Crockett. Sheriff Evans is visiting a local ranch. Can I help you?"

Not ideal, but perhaps he'd make more progress with a deputy. "I've arrived on the stage from San Francisco. I'm looking for my fiancée. Perhaps you've heard of her. Sophrona Thompson."

It took Cash a moment to place her. When he did, the entire story came back to him. "Can't place the name. Has she been in Splendor long?"

"Several weeks. She disappeared with a large amount of my money."

"I see. Do you have proof she stole the money?"

Drawing himself up to his full height didn't intimidate the deputy as he'd hoped. "My word should be sufficient."

"That's something you'll have to discuss with the sheriff. I can tell you he's real picky when it comes to arresting anyone without sufficient reason. Don't take offense, but your word isn't worth much here in Montana, Mr. Crockett."

Feeling as if he'd been slapped, Ezra held back a sharp retort. He told himself no one knew him out this way. The deputy didn't know he was an important man who could make or break someone with a few words spoken to the right people.

"When will the sheriff return?"

“Could be later tonight. It would be better if you came by tomorrow morning.”

Grabbing the satchels, Ezra moved toward the door. “I’ll be back tomorrow.”

Cash followed him at a distance until Ezra entered the St. James. Returning to the jail, he wrote a quick message to Gabe before mounting his horse for the short trip to the MacLaren ranch.

The men’s whoops and hollers signaled their approach to the ranch. Sean heard them first, rushing out of the barn to open a gate to the nearest corral. The instant the last horse entered the holding pen, he shut the gate, then moved to a much smaller, adjoining corral.

Coming in from another direction, Travis and Wyatt wrestled the stallion toward the separate pen. Given enough room to gain speed, the stallion might be able to clear the fence. Sean understood this and hoped the smaller corral would be too tight for the intimidating steed.

“Sean. We wondered when you’d get here.” Thane slid to the ground, tugging his cousin into a hug. “Sure good to see you.”

“It took longer than expected to get away. Da didn’t want me to leave, but once Finley arrived from Scotland, it was all fine. He’s an entertaining lad.”

“Sean!” Bram picked him up off the ground before setting him down. “We thought you’d forgotten us, lad.”

"Nae. Everything had to be right for me to leave. Once the clan accepted Finley, I left. Be prepared, though. They're talking about coming out for a visit."

"Let them come," Bram said. "They are always welcome."

"Aye." Sean laughed. "Remember you said that when they arrive at your front door."

Wyatt and Travis joined them. After introductions, they turned toward the house in time to see Selina rushing toward them.

"You had good luck on your search." Hugging Bram, she looked over his shoulder at the horses. "And you came back with a magnificent stallion."

"Aye. Wyatt and Travis are responsible for getting him to the ranch. He's not happy about his capture," Bram said.

Travis glanced over his shoulder at the stallion. "Wyatt and I will ride over here to break him. If it's all right. We'll stay here tonight and start on him tomorrow. If we tame him first, the other horses will be easier to break."

"We have plenty of room. Bring your gear inside. I want to introduce you to Sadie and our two babes." Taking Bram's arm, she moved him several feet away from Vince. "Kevin showed up while you were gone."

"What? Where is he?"

Shushing him, she tugged him farther away. "He's not in good shape. Rest, eating a little, is all he's done since showing up dirty and without any clothes. Sean took care of him. We aren't sure he recognizes Sadie or me. He's in a separate bedroom from Vince, but you should get inside and be there when he finds Kevin."

Nodding, Bram walked to Vince. "Come inside with me. Thane, can you take care of my horse?"

"Sure. I'll take care of yours, too, Vince."

Brows drawn together in confusion, he thanked Thane before following Bram inside. "What's going on?"

While Travis and Wyatt took care of their horses, carrying their belongings inside, Thane untacked his own horse. Brushing him down, he kept watch on the trail from town.

Something about the stagecoach, and the man watching out the window, niggled at him. He knew the stage originated in Salt Lake City, and that many caught it after taking the train from San Francisco. The city where Sadie had escaped from a man who'd planned to control her through a forced marriage.

Shaking off the intense unease, Thane put his and Bram's horse in a pasture on the opposite side of the wild horse herd. Before he could start on Vince's, he caught sight of a lone rider coming from town. As he got closer, Thane saw it was Deputy Cash Coulter.

The look on Cash's face had Thane stepping around the horses to intercept the deputy. "Cash. Surprised to see you out here this late in the afternoon."

Dismounting, he didn't waste time. "A man came in on the afternoon stage. He's looking for Sadie. His name is Ezra Crockett. I don't believe the man plans to leave without her."

Chapter Twenty-Four

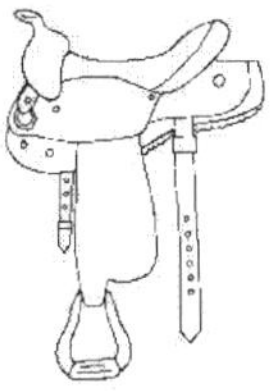

"It won't be much longer, Dante. We'll arrive in Splendor within a few hours." Cole had his arm around the boy, who'd been threatening to fall asleep since leaving Big Pine.

"Where will we live, Papa?" It hadn't been the first time he'd asked the question.

"I have a house in town."

"You said it's just one bedroom. Where will I sleep?"

"We'll move to a bigger house with two bedrooms. Until then, we'll make a bed for you on the floor."

Closing his eyes, this time, Dante lost his fight against sleep. Cole was glad for the respite. His adopted son had talked almost nonstop since leaving Cheyenne. He had no idea the young boy had so many questions. One answer led to another question until Cole had grown weary.

After a quick lunch in Big Pine and a courtesy hello to Sheriff Parker Sterling, they'd reboarded the stage for the last leg of the journey.

For the first time since leaving New York, Cole allowed his thoughts to fall on Martha. He hadn't contacted her since taking the stage east. It made no sense to continue a relationship when he didn't know what the future would hold.

At the time, his oldest sister had been mysteriously quiet about the reason she required his presence at the family mansion. He'd gotten no answers when he'd arrived in New York. Not until a few days before his plan to return west did his sister open up.

Would Martha understand a young man's earnest offer to take on the responsibility of a young boy? Cole hardly understood it himself.

He'd been young, traveling the west with no intention of returning east when a chance encounter with Evelyn Anderson ended in the offer. Cole had fallen hard for the mother and her young son. When her parents arrived to sweep her back home, he'd scribbled the offer on a small piece of paper. Six years later, the paper had traveled full circle to his sister. Replaying the entire, short relationship with Evelyn and Dante, it was with disbelief he found himself an unmarried father at the grand old age of thirty.

Two issues stuck in Cole's mind. First, he wanted to renew his courtship of Martha. Second, he didn't want her to think his motive was to locate a mother for Dante.

Jarred by a severe pothole, he glanced down at the boy. Thankfully, he continued to sleep. Cole's gaze landed on the empty seat across from them. It was a rare event when the stage to Splendor wasn't full.

Glad for the quiet, he began formulating a plan to approach Martha. She'd been patient with him as he struggled with the decision to return east. Patient, even as he'd told her nothing about his reason for leaving. He'd never known a woman to ask so few questions. Then again, he'd never actually asked to court her. In his mind, that was what they were doing. In hers? He had no answer.

Ticking off in his mind what needed to be done in Splendor, his first task would be to speak with Gabe Evans. Enrolling him in school was another item, as was meeting with Noah about a larger house. Cole had to shop for food, buy a few more clothes, and start teaching his son to ride a horse.

"We're ten minutes out, Cole," the driver shouted.

Ten more minutes, then his life would change once again.

Ezra rushed breakfast, intent on meeting with the sheriff early. He'd present the affidavits from the police chief in San Francisco, two deputies who spotted Sophrona going through Ezra's office files, and from friends who spoke to her about the plan to steal money before leaving.

There wasn't a lawman anywhere who'd dismiss the documentation he'd so painstakingly fabricated. The obvious, that the sheriff would question the evidence, hadn't been considered.

Finishing the last bite of the delicious omelet, he swallowed the last of his coffee, tapped the napkin to his lips, and shoving the chair back, he froze. A broad hand had planted itself on his shoulder.

"Don't get up, Mr. Crockett." Gabe moved so Ezra could see him, holding out his hand. "My deputy told me you were looking for me. I'm Gabe Evans. Sheriff of Splendor."

Accepting the outstretched hand, Ezra nodded toward a chair. "Please, join me. Have you had breakfast?"

"I have."

"Coffee, Sheriff Evans?" The middle-aged server was already pouring. "Black, right?"

"Yes. Thank you, Thelma."

She refilled Ezra's cup without asking. "Let me know if you want anything else. Oh, and Nick Barnett was in earlier, asking after you."

"I'll stop by the Dixie before returning to the jail."

"Very good." Giving a brisk nod, she left the men alone.

"The food here is much better than I expected. Who owns the hotel and restaurant?"

"I own it with a partner."

Ezra's wide eyes signaled his surprise. "I wouldn't have thought a small town sheriff would know much about hotels."

"You could say it's in my blood, Mr. Crockett. So, explain to me why you believe Sadie stole from you?"

"I'll do more than that. I have signed documents from people who saw her steal the money or who she spoke to about taking my money and leaving." Opening a folio, he took out the affidavits, handing them to Gabe. "Here you are."

Carefully reviewing them, he noticed the similarity in the signatures, and the fact not one actually accused Sadie of stealing. Their recollections were less clear. Her friends mentioned her planning to leave with some of Ezra's money, but no one saw her take it. Not even the police officers who watched her through a window at Ezra's house.

The police chief's signature appeared to be identical to those of his officers, and even Sadie's friends. Noting the name of the police chief, Gabe determined sending the man a telegram would be smart.

"These are all helpful. May I keep them a few days?"

Shifting in his chair, Ezra frowned. "I was hoping we could arrest her today. I would like to return her to San Francisco to stand trial."

"If what you've shown me is accurate, perhaps she could be tried here in Splendor." Although Gabe knew San Francisco was the proper location.

"Nonsense. The witnesses are back home."

Tipping back his cup, Gabe drank the last of his coffee and stood. "I'll make sure these get back to you, Mr. Crockett. My advice is to not go anywhere near Sadie until I've spoken to her. Along with a local attorney."

Ezra shot up, his amicable manner disappearing. "An attorney? Why? The evidence you have is overwhelming."

"Everyone deserves to be represented, Mr. Crockett. I'd say the same if you were accused of stealing her family money."

Clearing his throat, his face turned an alarming red.

"Are you all right, Mr. Crockett?"

He waved a hand in the air. "Fine. Her family has no money to speak of."

Another fact Gabe would verify with the police chief.

"I should get back to the jail. Good to meet you." Holding out his hand, he waited until Ezra finally took it.

"Sheriff. When can we talk again?"

"Tomorrow after lunch. Come to the jail, and I'll take you to the boardinghouse restaurant. Great down home food." Gabe walked toward the door, then turned. "You'll love it."

MacLaren Ranch

"What are you doing, Sadie?" Thane looked through the open bedroom door to see her satchel filled with her belongings.

Without stopping, she gave him a look which would've caused others to leave her alone. "You heard Cash. Ezra is in town. He only would've made the long trip out here to force me back to San Francisco." Her hands shook as she tried to fold a skirt, dropping it on the ground. "I'm sure he's already spoken to the sheriff. Probably gave him false information about me. I can't wait around for Ezra to talk Gabe into arresting me."

Thane swept the skirt off the floor, folded it, placing it on the bed. "You've met Gabe more than once. Do you believe he's a man who fools easily? He isn't going to be taken in by Ezra's lies."

Taking her hand, he encouraged her to sit down on the edge of the bed, with him beside her. "You're overreacting."

"You don't know him. Once he's made up his mind about something, he doesn't rest until he gets what he wants."

Squeezing her hand, he placed it between his two larger ones. "Any man who'd send two gunslingers to force you back to San Francisco can't be trusted. That action alone indicates the kind of man Ezra is."

"So you know why I must leave."

"No, I don't. You will never be more protected than you are right here on the ranch. There are four men who aren't going to let one man take you away. If it weren't for Selina needing you to help with the twins, I'd hide you out in one of the caves on our ranch. He'd never find you there. But that wouldn't solve the problem. We take a stand against Ezra right here."

"Sadie. Thane. Are you two upstairs?" There was an urgency in Selina's voice neither could miss.

"We are. Do you need us?"

"Bram is outside talking to Sheriff Evans. I'm certain he'll bring him inside for coffee."

"We'll be right down." Thane stood, pulling Sadie up with him. "I believe there's a good chance he's here because of Ezra. Come on. Let's talk to him." Holding out his hand, he waited until she threaded her fingers with his. Bending down, he brushed a kiss across her cheek. "He's a fair man, Sadie. He'll know what to do."

They entered the kitchen at the same time Bram and Gabe entered from outside. After brief greetings, and Selina setting coffee in front of each of them, Gabe pulled out the documents from a pocket.

"Ezra Crockett and I spoke this morning. He gave me these, which he claims proves you stole from him before running away. I'd like you to read through them, Sadie."

"All right."

He slid the first one in front of her. "Take your time. I don't want you to miss anything."

The document in front of her spoke of how a few of her close friends had learned she was leaving San Francisco and planned to take some of Ezra's money with her. A slow burn turned into righteous anger with each sentence.

"I know the women mentioned, but we aren't friends. I never would've confided anything to them. The fact is, I told no one I was leaving. It would've been too easy for my plan to get back to Ezra or my parents."

"You're certain you didn't say anything to these women?" Gabe asked.

"Positive. No one knew, Sheriff." Sliding it back to him, she accepted the next one in the pile. It spoke of police officers watching her rifle through files in his office. The implication was she was looking for money.

"This never happened. It couldn't have. Ezra always locked his office and posted a guard in the hall. I was allowed in there exactly four times, and he was there each time. So was my chaperone."

"You had a chaperone?" Gabe asked.

"Oh, yes. An older woman who slept in the room next to mine. She had no idea I planned to leave, either."

"Did he have a safe in the office?" Gabe asked.

"I'm certain he did. Perhaps more than one. My parents gave me an allowance. I saved for months to have enough for train and stagecoach fare. Although, I did believe it would get me farther east than Splendor. If I planned to steal his money, it would've been more than enough to get me to at least Kansas City."

"This last one is a statement from the police chief. He states he heard you talking about leaving and taking money from Ezra." He handed her the paper.

She couldn't contain her laughter. "The police chief and Ezra can't stand each other. Not since Ezra funded an opponent's campaign to fire the chief. Ezra's man lost, which meant so did Ezra. Trust me, the police chief wouldn't sign anything such as this as a favor."

She picked up the stack, holding it out to Gabe before pulling it back.

"Wait. May I see the pages next to each other?"

Gabe nodded.

Studying them for several minutes, she shook her head. "The signatures look almost identical on all the documents. Are you sure they were signed by different people?" She glanced up to see a broad smile on Gabe's face.

"I'm not sure at all, Sadie. Not at all."

Chapter Twenty-Five

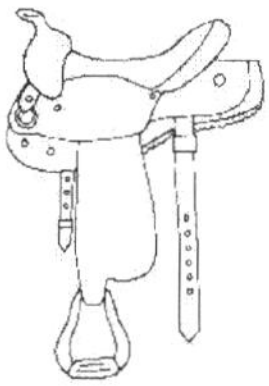

The return telegram Gabe received from the police chief in San Francisco answered his questions. The man hadn't seen or heard anything about the reason behind Sadie's leaving, nor did he know about missing money. The missive ended with the chief's warning about being real careful when dealing with Ezra Crockett.

The man had gone a step further, sending a second telegram later before lunch saying none of the officers he spoke with would admit to seeing Sadie in Ezra's office. Gabe had decided not to try to locate the friends of Sadie's who Ezra had signed affidavits from. He expected they'd be as fraudulent as the others.

The question was what to do about the lies Ezra was spreading. While eating breakfast at McCall's that morning, he'd overheard a couple talking about a woman suspected of stealing money. They heard she was hiding out in Splendor. Although her name wasn't mentioned, Gabe knew they referred to Sadie.

He had to stop Ezra, and send him back to San Francisco. Forcing him wouldn't work. Men such as him would use connections to contact the governor, enlisting his help. Gabe didn't want to play politics, but would if pushed.

There was always the option to arrest him for providing false statements. It would require sworn affidavits from the sheriff, and Sadie would have to appear in front of the circuit judge, along with Ezra. If found guilty, Gabe had no idea what penalty the judge would impose.

The jail door opened. Although early, he expected Ezra to walk inside. Instead, Cole Santori ushered a young boy into the jail.

"I heard you were back." Gabe walked around his desk to pump his deputy's hand. "Good to have you back. Who's this?"

"My son. Well, adopted son, Dante. Dante, this is my boss, Sheriff Evans."

He dutifully held out his hand to Gabe. "Hello, sir."

"It's a pleasure meeting you, Dante. How old are you?"

"I'm eight."

"You're pretty tall for eight. Are you certain you aren't twelve?"

Dante smiled, looking up at Cole. "I'm just eight."

"Would it be all right if Dante looked at the wanted posters while we talk?"

"Good idea." Gabe opened a drawer, pulling out a stack of papers. "You can sit here, Dante. Let me know if you see anyone you recognize."

"All right." He climbed into the chair. Starting with the first poster, he studied it before setting it aside.

"Let's talk over here." Gabe pulled a chair toward the stove, and poured two cups of coffee. Cole took the cup Gabe offered before sitting down. "I take it this is a new relationship." Gabe tilted his head toward Dante.

Cole explained in a quiet voice, looking over at Dante every few minutes. Finishing, he set the empty cup aside and opened his palms.

"I made the offer and she took me up on it."

"You're good with it, Cole?"

"Yes, I am. Noah has a two bedroom house I can move into by the end of the week. I still have to take Dante to the school and introduce him to Rose Keenan."

"That's right. You probably don't know about the changes. They won't affect you and Dante, though."

Cole's brows shot up. "What changes?"

"Ruth Paige, Martha van Plew, and a few other church women, including my wife, Lena, were able to open a home for orphans south of town. I don't recall the exact count, but believe there are six to eight children there. Until they find a permanent house manager, Martha is fulfilling the position. Rose Keenan is teaching the orphans, as well as the students in town. Amelia Newhall left her position at the Eagle's Nest to become the cook. Both Rose and Amelia help with activities and live at the home. The women did a real fine job putting it all together."

Cole heard all Gabe said, though his mind had locked on Martha's name. "Miss van Plew manages the home?"

"Until a replacement may be found. Too bad. She's an excellent administrator. You might want to take Dante out there and introduce him." Gabe drained the last of the coffee in his cup, setting it aside. "You'll probably want to work days, right?"

"If possible."

"It is. When do you want to start?"

Cole glanced again at his son, who busied himself with the posters. "I need a few days to get Dante settled and enrolled in school."

"Will Monday give you enough time?"

"Plenty, Gabe. I appreciate it."

"You're a fine deputy, Cole. I'm glad to have you back."

MacLaren Ranch

Vince sat on a chair in Kevin's room, listening to his brother snore. He'd been sleeping at least sixteen hours each day since his return, eating little. Doctor Drake Ralston had ridden out to give his opinion and check for infections. To everyone's surprise, he was malnourished, still disoriented, but otherwise healthy.

"All he needs is rest, food, and support from his family," the doctor had said. Like others who visited the MacLarens, Drake believed Vince and Kevin were part of the family, and in all ways that counted, they were.

Reaching out, he took hold of his brother's hand. The once brawny hand and arm was so slim, Vince could have wrapped his fingers around it.

"Considering what all he must have been through, Kev's in decent shape." Selina held Audrey, her features full of empathy. "He'll be good as new soon."

"I know. It's just hard to see him like this."

"I heard you."

Seeing his brother's eyes open, Vince dropped his hand. "I thought you were asleep."

"Who can sleep with you talking?" Turning onto his back, Kevin tried to prop himself up without success.

"I'll help you." Vince grabbed an extra pillow, helping his brother lean against it and the wall at the head of the bed.

"That's good. Thanks."

"How about some soup, Kev? Sadie made it this morning."

"Sadie?" Lifting his hand, he scratched his head.

"She wasn't here long when you disappeared," Vince said.

"I remember her now." He looked at Selina. "I'd be grateful for some soup."

"It'll just take a minute." Handing Audrey to Vince, she dashed downstairs, returning a couple minutes later with soup and a slice of bread with butter on a tray. "Here you are."

Taking Audrey from Vince, she turned to leave. "Call out if you want more. Bram, Thane, and Sadie are out with the herd. I expect them back anytime."

She took a quick look behind her before heading downstairs. Smiling as she watched the brothers talk, she knew everything would be all right.

"Are you sure you'll be all right?" Bram was anxious to get back to the house. Selina had been home with the twins all day. Even with Vince helping when not outside, the babes were a lot of work. "Why don't you ride back with me?"

Thane shoved his hat back on his head. "Thanks, Bram. We want to take a little more time out here. We'll be back soon."

"All right. See you at the house."

Watching as he rode off, Thane slid to the ground before helping Sadie down. "Feel like walking?"

"After being in that saddle most of the day, I'd love to walk."

Taking her hand, they walked in silence for a long time, skirting the edges of the herd as the cattle grazed.

"I know you're nervous about Ezra being in Splendor."

"He's a beast, Thane."

"We have to trust Gabe to take care of the legal stuff. Once he does, Ezra won't have a choice but to give up and return to San Francisco."

"You don't know him like I do. He's not a good loser."

"He won't have a choice, sweetheart."

"Ezra will always allow himself a choice. He doesn't let circumstances stop him. If pushed, he'll fight back."

"You never did plan to marry him, did you?"

She tugged on his hand to stop. "Of course not. The man is a vile monster."

Leaning down, he drew her in for a kiss, then wrapped his arms around her. "Good," he breathed against her hair.

"Good that he's vile, or that I never wanted to marry him?"

"Funny." He continued toward the sound of water running along the nearby creek. "This is one of my favorite places. I discovered it not long after we moved out from California. This is where I want to have the ceremony."

Scrunching her brows, she looked up at him. "Ceremony?"

"Our wedding, Sadie." Stopping, he turned her toward him. "I love you. I can't imagine not having you here with me. If you feel the same, marry me."

"Marry..."

"Yes. Stay with me on the ranch. Build a life and family with me."

"Marry you." The whispered words became more real each time she spoke them. "You love me?"

"You didn't know? I must've done a terrible job of showing you."

"I'm certain you didn't do a terrible job, Mr. MacLaren. Sophrona is just a lousy listener. Aren't you, Soph?"

Both turned at the man's voice, Sadie's face draining of color. "Ezra..."

"Of course, my dear." He walked to within ten feet of them, his gun pointed at them. "You were right when you said I am a poor loser. I'm still considering your description of me as a vile monster." He pointed a finger at her. "You may be correct."

Chapter Twenty-Six

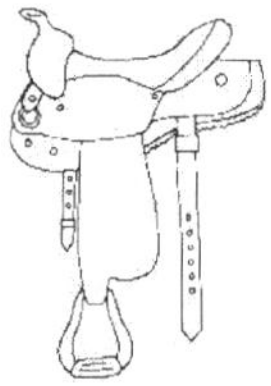

"Hey, Sheriff." Bernie Griggs bounced into the jail, glad to find Gabe at his desk. "You have an emergency telegram." He waved the paper in the air a few times before holding it out. Noticing they were alone, he still lowered his voice. "From the police chief in San Francisco."

"Thanks, Bernie."

"Do you want me to wait for a reply?"

"Sure. Have some coffee while you wait." Gabe nodded to the stove.

"You bet, Sheriff. Everyone knows you have the best coffee in town."

"Because it's what they use at the Eagle's Nest."

"Sure. Sure. We all know that." Cradling the cup with both hands, Bernie savored the coffee with his usual huge smile.

Across the room, Gabe wasn't savoring the telegram. "Did you read this, Bernie?"

"Of course. I read all of them."

"Have you told anybody about it?"

Setting down the cup, Bernie jumped to his feet, indignant at the accusation. "I'd never do that."

"Sorry, but I had to ask."

"I saw him ride out of town earlier today."

"Which direction?"

"Toward the MacLaren ranch."

MacLaren Ranch

"What are you planning, Ezra?" Sadie tried to keep her voice even, doubting she'd succeeded.

"Well, my dear, I haven't decided. You and I will marry, of course. That means we'll have to leave this lovely hamlet in Montana and return to San Francisco. We simply can't be married in such a hostile environment."

"She isn't going anywhere with you, Ezra."

"You are a brave man, Mr. MacLaren. You have no hope of getting away, yet you play the protector to our distressed damsel."

Sadie scoffed at his choice of words. "Have you ever thought about how ridiculous you sound?"

Eyes narrowing, Ezra waved the gun in the air. "I'd warn you to be careful, Sophrona. I'm not at my best today."

Thane reached out, gripping her arm before she could agitate Ezra anymore. "Stay calm. We'll get out of this."

"How?"

"Uh-uh." He waggled the gun back and forth. "No whispering, you two."

"He *is* crazy," she muttered.

"Aye," he mumbled against her ear. "How did you find us, Crockett?"

"I followed you from the house earlier today. No one will be looking for me, or for you two."

"Don't be so sure. When we don't get back for supper, Bram, Sean, and Vince will come looking."

"By then, Sadie and I will be long gone. And you, well...you'll no longer matter."

"You aren't going to do anything to hurt Thane." Sadie reached out, grabbing Thane's hand.

"That's right. The two of you plan to marry. Two young lovers who have no future. Such a sad event." He walked around them, motioning the gun toward their mounts. "Now, get to your horses. We're leaving here."

Thane wanted to focus Ezra's attention away from Sadie and on him. It surprised him the man hadn't tried to relieve him of his gun.

"Where are we going?" Sadie kept within a few inches of Thane.

"You and I, my dear, are traveling back to San Francisco. Alas, Mr. MacLaren won't be making the trip with us." He stopped next to their horses. "I'd appreciate it if you'd drop your gun on the ground, Mr. MacLaren. Along with your shotgun." Ezra nodded toward the scabbard.

Keeping the gun trained on Thane, Ezra waited until he'd swung into the saddle, then mounted his own horse. "Now you, my dear. Bring the horse over here."

Her mind raced with ideas for getting away, but all would end if Ezra shot Thane. The man truly was crazy.

She'd known his mind didn't work the same as everyone else's, but she'd never considered him a murderer. Then again, Sadie hadn't considered herself a killer until circumstances ended with the deaths of Ezra's two men. Everette Wardell and Hugo Platt should never have drawn their weapons on Thane and Bram.

Mounting her horse, Sadie stayed within feet of Ezra. Perhaps she could distract him long enough for Thane to draw the gun he kept in his right boot.

"All right. It's time to finish this."

Splendor

Gabe counted the number of deputies ready to ride with him to the MacLaren ranch. Five. He didn't need many. Caleb Covington, Beau Davis, and the newest deputies, Morgan Wheeler, Jonas Taylor, and Tucker Nolan.

"Everyone clear on what we're doing?"

The five nodded their heads at the same time they checked their six-shooters, shotguns, and rifles. If Ezra Crockett was the only threat, the men were over armed. Gabe figured better to err on the safe side.

"All right. Let's head out." Taking the lead, he selected a direct route to the ranch.

Gabe had read the telegram from the police chief in San Francisco several times. It wasn't incriminating by itself, but combined with Ezra's other, potentially illegal actions, it put him under suspicion for an additional crime. A crime the police chief had an intense interest in discussing with Ezra. He'd have a great deal of explaining to do upon his return to the west coast.

The immediate reason Gabe and his men were riding to the MacLaren ranch, in addition to the telegram, was to confirm Ezra posed no immediate danger. The throbbing in Gabe's stomach indicated they might already be too late.

Rounding a bend toward the top of a hill, Gabe and his men held up. Below them, in a rolling valley, grazed the MacLaren herd. Three people rode to the south, causing Gabe's chest to squeeze. Thane, Sadie, and if he weren't mistaken, Ezra Crockett. Even from this distance, Gabe could see the gun trained on Thane's back.

Thane kept his gaze moving as they put distance between them and the herd. He knew the area well, aware of a string of caves less than a quarter mile away. He wasn't sure what good they'd do him and Sadie now.

"Where are you taking us, Ezra?"

"I'm getting you away from the house. That way, no one will hear the shot."

Her throat tightened. "What shot?"

"Come now, Sophrona. You don't believe I can leave Mr. MacLaren alive, do you? I plan for us to ride back to Splendor in time for tomorrow's stage to Salt Lake City."

"If I go with you willingly, there's no reason to kill him, Ezra. We'll ride away now and take tomorrow's stage. I'll marry you as soon as we reach San Francisco."

Throwing his head back, a hysterical laugh burst from Ezra's throat. "You've had a good deal of time to return to me, my dear. I'm taking no chances this time. With Mr. MacLaren gone, your choices will shrink to one. Returning with me to San Francisco. Your parents are quite worried, you know. You shouldn't have put them through so much stress."

Sadie ignored the rebuke. Her parents hadn't cared about her welfare since sending her and a chaperone to live with Ezra. Their reasons were their own. She suspected they had more to do with being associated with an influential member of San Francisco society, than the welfare of their daughter. In the position she and Thane were in now, going back with him might be the only way to save either of their lives.

"You're right. Still, killing Thane isn't necessary. You don't want to be remembered as a murderer."

Ezra's return laughter put her on edge.

"We'll marry as soon as we reach San Francisco. Or we can marry in Salt Lake City, or even Splendor." Sadie hated the pleading tone of her voice. She'd do anything to save Thane's life.

"It won't be long now," was Ezra's solemn response.

Sadie was afraid their options were quickly narrowing.

Cash and Beau returned from a scouting trip ordered by Gabe, reining up when they reached the group.

"Ezra is alone, Gabe," Cash said. "He has a gun on Thane. We couldn't get close enough to hear what was said, but my guess is he plans to kill Thane and take off with Sadie."

Nodding, the sheriff considered his next steps. "I'm certain you're right."

"We don't have much time before the sun sets. He's going to want to head back to town before then," Beau said.

Gabe divided the group into thirds, sending Cash and Beau to the right, Morgan and Jonas would approach to the left, and Tucker, who'd ride with Gabe, would approach from behind.

"There are a string of caves ahead of where they're riding." Cash pointed to the south. "He's going to shoot Thane and leave him there."

Gabe thought that over, deciding to send Cash and Beau ahead instead of coming in from the right. "Do what you have to do to save Thane and Sadie."

Touching the brims of their hats, the two whirled their horses around to intercept Ezra.

Ezra's behavior became more erratic the closer they came to the caves. His head whipped from one direction to another, watching for anything that would hinder his plans.

Less than fifty yards from the entrance to the first cave, their horses became agitated, dancing around. Thane thought he understood the reason.

"Keep him distracted, Sadie." He hoped she'd heard his whispered words. When her horse slowed so she could come alongside Ezra, Thane leaned to his right, going for the gun slipped into his right boot.

Long fingers wrapped around the handle. Hesitating a moment when it caught on his trousers, he tugged it free.

Riding through an opening between two large boulders, Thane tensed. The hairs on the back of his neck stood up.

As the hand gripping the gun pulled it up and out of the boot, a dark, tan form flashed before him. "Sadie, get down."

In a fluid movement, Thane swiveled, leveled the gun, and fired. One, two, three times, before the form let out a scream, twisted in the air, and landed on the hard ground. Beneath him was the motionless body of Ezra Crockett.

Chapter Twenty-Seven

Gabe and his deputies arrived minutes after the mountain lion trapped Ezra. Unfortunately, Crockett survived. The cat didn't.

Before Ezra could regain consciousness, Cash and Beau had checked for broken bones and other injuries. They assumed there were wounds they couldn't see. Internal and unable to be treated. No one would voice their thoughts on whether he'd make it to trial.

Gabe and Tucker accompanied Thane and Sadie to the ranch house while the others delivered Ezra to Splendor's clinic. Though no one thought he'd wake up soon, Morgan and Jonas agreed to stay with the doctor in case the deranged killer fooled them.

After receiving the telegram from the police chief about Ezra's illegal activities, including the possible murder of his business partner, the story Thane and Sadie described didn't surprise Gabe. Nor did the fact he'd planned to kill the younger MacLaren.

He and Jonas left after Selina insisted they stay for supper. Gabe planned to contact the U.S. Marshal service about transporting Ezra back to San Francisco for the trial of his murdered business partner. First, he'd stand trial in Splendor for the planned murder of Thane.

Standing on the kitchen stoop, watching as Gabe and Jonas disappeared into the distance, Thane took Sadie's hand.

"Let's walk."

The night had stayed warm with a slight cooling breeze coming from the north. Her hand in his felt right. They were both recovering from the encounter with Ezra and the unanticipated attack by the mountain lion.

Stepping into the barn, Thane took a moment to light a lantern before leading her out the back. Tonight, the corral was empty, allowing them to walk the area in silence.

Several minutes passed before Thane stopped, tugging Sadie to him. "I don't want you to return to San Francisco."

Looking down at their joined hands, she gave a small shake of her head. "I don't know what's best. We've been through so much. Still, we haven't known each other long."

He knew Sadie was right. Their time together had been short and eventful. Most couples wouldn't experience half of what they'd been through in their brief lives.

"Perhaps it would be best if you did return to your parents. Being back home may help you decide what's best for you."

She hadn't expected him to encourage her to leave. "Is that what you want?"

"You know what I want, Sadie."

Pursing her lips, her gaze latched onto the darkening sky. "It's so beautiful here. Do you think I'm strong enough to make a life on a ranch?"

"It's not what I believe, Sadie. It's about what you want. In here." He touched her head. "And in here." He pointed to her heart. "I can't make that decision for you."

Sadie woke the following morning to a beautiful, late spring day. The horrors of the afternoon before had given way to a serene acceptance of the life she wanted. It wasn't a return to San Francisco.

Throwing off the covers, she performed her ablutions, dressed, and hurried downstairs. Kevin sat at the table with Connor settled in one arm. Selina had tucked Audrey against her side while finishing a plate of eggs and bacon.

"Good morning." Making her way across the kitchen, she picked up a piece of toast. "Where is everyone?"

"If you mean Bram, Thane, Vince, and Sean, they're working with the wild horses." Selina nodded toward the barn. "They hope to break at least four of them by the end of the day."

"Do you mind if I, um..."

Selina smiled. "Go ahead, Sadie. I'm sure Thane will be glad to see you."

"What about Audrey and Connor?"

"I'm pretty sure Kev and I can take care of them."

"Well, if you're sure."

Selina waved a hand in the air. "Go."

Not wasting another minute, Sadie set down what was left of her uneaten toast before rushing outside. Shouts drew her to the other side of the barn.

In the middle of the pasture, Thane and Bram worked with one of the horses. Vince and Sean stood on the lowest rung of the fence, watching.

Ever since waking up, Sadie felt a sense of calm. Unlike a few hours earlier, the idea of staying in Splendor felt right.

She was ready to burst with the need to speak with Thane. Overnight, her mood had changed from uncertainty to excitement. Sadie had come to a decision, and she couldn't wait to share it with Thane.

Glancing over his shoulder, he spotted her and waved before turning back to the mare they were taming. She didn't know how much time passed before he handed the lines to Vince and jogged toward her, his smile melting whatever hesitancy might remain.

"Good morning, Sadie." Joining her outside the fence, he ran a hand along her arm before turning to watch Vince and Bram.

"Morning, Thane. Selina said you're breaking horses?"

"We hope to have at least four today. We should be able to finish within a few days. Then we'll need to search for more wild horses to fulfil the contracts."

Focusing on what was happening in the pasture, he didn't sense the change before she wrapped her arms around his neck.

"I love you, Thane."

The unexpected announcement surprised him. "You..." he stuttered.

"I love you."

Slipping his hand around her waist, he looked down at her. "Which means?"

"If you're still interested, I will marry you."

Laughing, Thane picked Sadie up, twirling her in a circle before setting her down for a passionate kiss. "Sadie, love. I will always be interested."

Cole sat on the bench seat of the wagon, with Dante beside him, the boy's attention focused on the trail to the home for orphans. He'd been full of questions when they'd left town. By halfway there, he'd fallen silent.

It had taken longer to get settled in the larger house rented from Noah than anticipated. Cole had purchased furniture for another bedroom, plus several more items for the kitchen.

Dressed in a new shirt, trousers, boots, and hat, Dante looked as if he'd been born to the west.

Stomach roiling, Cole couldn't recall the last time he'd been so nervous about talking to a woman. He was sure Martha knew of his return to Splendor. Had probably heard about Dante. Cole hoped she'd give him time to explain before forming her own conclusions.

They arrived at the large house in time to see her standing on the wraparound porch. She watched the children play in the front yard. At first, she gave no indication of recognizing him.

It wasn't until he stopped the wagon, helping Dante down, that a smile played at the corners of her mouth. Walking down the steps, she stopped several feet away.

"Hello, Cole. It has been a while. I heard you were back in town. I also heard you didn't arrive alone."

"Hello, Martha." He didn't lean forward to brush a kiss across her cheek. Instead, he rested a hand on Dante's shoulder, drawing him forward. "You're right. It has been a while."

"Who do we have here?"

"This is Dante Columbus Santori. My son."

Epilogue

One month later...

The wedding of Thane MacLaren and Sadie Thompson took place exactly where he'd hoped. Next to the creek, not far from the house. It seemed the entire town showed up to hear their marriage vows and celebrate.

Selina and the women from Redemption's Edge designed and sewed a gorgeous dress of white tulle and silk. The cuffs and collar were decorated with tiny pearls, and Rachel Pelletier had loaned Sadie a string of pearls given to her by her husband, Dax.

The church women made a delicious feast of roast duck, beef, and chicken, along with dried fruit, boiled cabbage and tomatoes, vegetables with lamb soup, fruit cake, and brown sugar pudding.

Stan Petermann, the owner of the general store, and three other businessmen provided spirited music, which kept everyone dancing.

Throughout it all, Thane and Sadie never lost their smiles. They welcomed everyone, and made sure each guest knew how much their presence meant.

The big surprise happened when three MacLaren couples from California arrived the night before the ceremony. Colin and Sarah, Brodie and Maggie, and Quinn and Emma stayed at the St. James, riding out in the morning to help with the celebration.

Cole stood to the side with several other deputies, watching Dante play with the children he'd met at school and at the orphan home. The children at the home had become his closest friends, though he was getting to know more of the children in town and at neighboring ranches.

Across the way, Martha spent most of her time with her close friend, Angela, and her husband, fellow deputy Shane Banderas. The two employees of the orphan home, Amelia Newhall and Rose Keenan, along with Morgan Wheeler and Jonas Taylor, stayed close.

Cole's attempts to get Martha to dance, or even talk to him, were ignored. She'd smile, be her usual, pleasant self, but made sure there was always distance between them.

He knew it all had to do with how he'd treated her before leaving for New York. The days and weeks he hadn't come by to take her to lunch or supper. Cole couldn't blame her. She deserved better than what he'd given her.

Then there was Dante. They'd been interrupted at the home for orphans when he'd attempted to explain the boy and how Cole had come to adopt him.

That would be a difficult conversation. He'd fallen in love with Dante's mother, Evelyn. Would've married her if she hadn't been whisked back to Baltimore by her parents.

Because of a tragic accident which took Evelyn's life, as well as those of her parents, Cole was Dante's legal guardian. He hoped Martha would allow him to explain the entire situation sooner rather than later.

For now, her efforts were centered on managing the home, doing what was best for the children, and locating a qualified administrator. He respected her dedication, and hoped she understood his desire to be the best father possible for a boy who'd lost his family.

Learn about upcoming books in the **Redemption Mountain** series at **www.shirleendavies.com**.

Enjoy the Redemption Mountain books? Here's another series you might want to read. **MacLarens of Boundary Mountain** historical western romance series. You can find it at **www.shirleendavies.com**.

If you want to keep current on all my preorders, new releases, and other happenings, sign up for my newsletter at **http://www.shirleendavies.com/contact-me.html**

A Note from Shirleen

Thank you for taking the time to read **Captive Dawn**! If you enjoyed it, please consider telling your friends or posting a short review. Word of mouth is an author's best friend and much appreciated.

I care about quality, so if you find something in error, please contact me via email at **shirleen@shirleendavies.com**

Books by Shirleen Davies

Find all of my books at:
https://www.shirleendavies.com/books.html

Contemporary Western Romance Series

MacLarens of Fire Mountain

Second Summer, Book One
Hard Landing, Book Two
One More Day, Book Three
All Your Nights, Book Four
Always Love You, Book Five
Hearts Don't Lie, Book Six
No Getting Over You, Book Seven
'Til the Sun Comes Up, Book Eight
Foolish Heart, Book Nine

Macklins of Whiskey Bend

Thorn, Book One
Del, Book Two
Boone, Book Three
Kell, Book Four
Zane, Book Five
Josh, Book Six, Coming Next in the Series!

Cowboys of Whistle Rock Ranch

The Cowboy's Road Home, Book One
The Cowboy's False Start, Book Two
The Cowboy's Second Chance Family, Book Three
The Cowboy's Final Ride, Book Four
The Cowboy's Surprise Reunion, Book Five, Coming Next in the Series!

Historical Western Romance Series

Redemption Mountain

Redemption's Edge, Book One
Wildfire Creek, Book Two
Sunrise Ridge, Book Three
Dixie Moon, Book Four
Survivor Pass, Book Five
Promise Trail, Book Six
Deep River, Book Seven
Courage Canyon, Book Eight
Forsaken Falls, Book Nine
Solitude Gorge, Book Ten
Rogue Rapids, Book Eleven
Angel Peak, Book Twelve
Restless Wind, Book Thirteen
Storm Summit, Book Fourteen
Mystery Mesa, Book Fifteen
Thunder Valley, Book Sixteen

A Very Splendor Christmas, Holiday Novella, Book Seventeen
Paradise Point, Book Eighteen,
Silent Sunset, Book Nineteen
Rocky Basin, Book Twenty
Captive Dawn, Book Twenty-One
Whisper Lake, Book Twenty-Two, Coming Next in the Series!

MacLarens of Fire Mountain

Tougher than the Rest, Book One
Faster than the Rest, Book Two
Harder than the Rest, Book Three
Stronger than the Rest, Book Four
Deadlier than the Rest, Book Five
Wilder than the Rest, Book Six

MacLarens of Boundary Mountain

Colin's Quest, Book One,
Brodie's Gamble, Book Two
Quinn's Honor, Book Three
Sam's Legacy, Book Four
Heather's Choice, Book Five
Nate's Destiny, Book Six
Blaine's Wager, Book Seven
Fletcher's Pride, Book Eight
Bay's Desire, Book Nine
Cam's Hope, Book Ten

Romantic Suspense

Eternal Brethren, Military Romantic Suspense

Steadfast, Book One
Shattered, Book Two
Haunted, Book Three
Untamed, Book Four
Devoted, Book Five
Faithful, Book Six
Exposed, Book Seven
Undaunted, Book Eight
Resolute, Book Nine
Unspoken, Book Ten
Defiant, Book Eleven

Peregrine Bay, Romantic Suspense

Reclaiming Love, Book One
Our Kind of Love, Book Two

Find all of my books at:
https://www.shirleendavies.com/books.html

About Shirleen

Shirleen Davies writes romance—historical, contemporary, and romantic suspense. She grew up in Southern California, attended Oregon State University, and has degrees from San Diego State University and the University of Maryland. During the day she provides consulting services to small and mid-sized businesses. But her real passion is writing emotionally charged stories of flawed people who find redemption through love and acceptance. She now lives with her husband in a beautiful town in northern Arizona.

I love to hear from my readers.

Send me an email: shirleen@shirleendavies.com
Visit my Website: https://www.shirleendavies.com/
Sign up to be notified of New Releases:
https://www.shirleendavies.com/contact/
Follow me on Amazon:
http://www.amazon.com/author/shirleendavies
Follow me on BookBub:
https://www.bookbub.com/authors/shirleen-davies

Other ways to connect with me:

Facebook Author Page:
http://www.facebook.com/shirleendaviesauthor
Pinterest: http://pinterest.com/shirleendavies

Instagram:
https://www.instagram.com/shirleendavies_author/
TikTok: shirleendavies_author
Twitter: www.twitter.com/shirleendavies

Avalanche Ranch Press, LLC
PO Box 12618
Prescott, AZ 86304